A change is gonna come. Young African-Americans will soon take their rightful places, helping America revolutionize politics, church and community. The year 2008 will be a throwback to the 1960's, when young African Americans took a stand for a positive change in society.

I0638924

Hot Topics

The 1ˢᵗ Black President of the U.S.

Respect

Gangs

Dr. W.E.B. Dubois

The "N" Word

Oprah Winfrey

Hip-Hop

Desegregating Schools

A.I.D.S.

Beyoncé & Jay-Z

Drug Abuse

Building Relationships

Politics & Voting

Church & State

Economic Empowerment

Langston Hughes

Imprisonment

Booker T. Washington

Black Youth

Emmett Till

NAACP

Social Responsibility

Giving

Wife-y vs. Wife

Black Organizations

The Birmingham Church Burning

Civil Rights

Immigration

Black Leadership

Family

Passing the Torch

50 cent

Hot Topics

Black Vernacular	Scripture Reading
Jena 6	Marital Sex
Don Imus	Characters named after Biblical people
Brown vs. Board of Education	"The Rapture"
No Child Left Behind	Husband & Wife
Electoral Vote	Faith
Rockefeller Law	Believing
Outsourcing	Preventative Programs
Nat Turner	Learning the Bible
Bill Clinton	Healing
Bishop Edgar A. Love	Gratefulness
Sharecropping	Pregnancy
Al Sharpton	Life & Death
Jesse Jackson	Heaven & Hell
Bill Cosby	Revenge
Freedom Fighters	Prosperity
Baby Boomers	Taking the Lead
Microwave Generation	Character Assassination
Generation X	Friendship
Not-for-profit Organizations	How to get SAVED
Perseverance	Self Hate
Love	Racism
	Power of Words

Truth of the Matter

A Change Is Gonna Come

Psalm 51: 6 "Behold, you desire Truth *in the inner being; make me therefore to know wisdom in my inmost heart."*

By

Bruce K. Davis Jr.

Published by, Bruce K. Davis, Jr.

Bruce K. Davis, Jr.

Table of Contents

Bruce K. Davis, Jr.

Introduction

Philippians 4:13 "I can do all things through Christ who strengthens me."

As a young Christian, God heard my cries and gave me the strength to face any challenge in school, the community, in church, or with my family by changing me.

I pray after you (young people) have finished reading these commentaries; it will spark something in you to want to continue to grow in Christ. I pray it will inspire you to want to write your own stories or poetry and read others especially the Bible. I pray, you are so moved by the message God gave to me that you will entrench yourself in school activities and in helping improve your community. I pray that our young generation will start a political movement in the 2008 election that will have the same impact of the youth of the 1960's. I pray that our families recover from generations of AIDS and crack cocaine. I pray the Rockefeller Law which locked away our fathers; the diseases that plagued our mothers; and the Welfare system that has left our families on the brink of extinction, is reformed and you are empowered to make changes through Christ. I pray that my gift to express myself in writing will not anger or inflame a young nation but instead will make you think. May this book be as therapeutic for you to read as it was for me to write. I pray for a change in our young people's lives. I pray for our salvation. I pray that my peers are so tired of struggling that they find the courage to wage war on a system that keeps us from feeding our families, educating our children and governing our communities. I pray other young leaders may realize their potential to make a difference. Stand up for your community. Stand up for your legacy. Make a change.

I pray when I'm of a mature age, I will be able to smoothly swallow the medicine I prescribe for others. I pray my elders will have a better understanding of our young Christians and our young Christian will respect the knowledge and wisdom of our elders.

Our Future…

Our Responsibility.

Truth Of The Matter
1 Peter 5:1-10 <u>To Elders and Young Men</u>

1. To the elders among you, I appeal as a fellow elder, a witness of Christ's sufferings and one who also will share in the glory to be revealed:

2. Be shepherds of God's flock that is under your care, serving as overseers—not because you must, but because you are willing, as God wants you to be; not greedy for money, but eager to serve;

3. Not lording it over those entrusted to you, but being examples to the flock.

4. And when the Chief Shepherd appears, you will receive the crown of glory that will never fade away.

5. Young men, in the same way be submissive to those who are older. All of you, clothe yourselves with humility toward one another, because, "God opposes the proud but gives grace to the humble."

6. Humble yourselves, therefore, under God's mighty hand, that he may lift you up in due time.

7. Cast all your anxiety on him because he cares for you.

8. Be self-controlled and alert. Your enemy the devil prowls around like a roaring lion looking for someone to devour.

9. Resist him, standing firm in the faith, because you know that your Brothers throughout the world are undergoing the same kind of sufferings.

10. And the God of all grace, who called you to his eternal glory in Christ, after you have suffered a little while, will himself restore you and make you strong, firm and steadfast.

11. To him be the power for ever and ever. Amen.

Bruce K. Davis, Jr.

IN HONORABLE MEMORY OF

James Counts

Artist, Community Activist

Roosevelt, New York

THE LONG ISLAND BLACK ARTISTS ASSOCIATION was co-founded in 1968 by James Counts and three other artists. The purpose of the association is to help African-American artists find a conduit for the exhibition of their work. To that end, it has continually sought new venues for exhibiting the work of its members locally, nationally and internationally and has also encouraged the artist's individual efforts to find recognition.

"Young man, if you and I are ever to make it, we have to help each other. I have lived long enough to have the wisdom and knowledge; you are young and have the will power and energy to fight. We cannot fight each other because I know what it took to get there. So, we have to help one another. I got your back [Young man], if you have [an old man's] back."

Thank you for explaining Willie Lynch to us as the younger generation.

IN HONORABLE MEMORY OF

Hykiem Coney

Gangster to Gospel

Gang Activist

Hempstead, New York

At the age of fifteen, Coney was the founder of a Hempstead gang called the Outlaws, which was part of the bloods.

"We didn't think that it was going to grow as big as it did," Coney said of the gang he helped found. The Outlaws started with weekly meetings every Friday, where girls would be initiated by having sex and boys would be beaten for a pre-determined amount of time. The gang's violence progressed to the point where members began using guns, according to Coney. "I actually shot somebody myself, and the guy shot me when I was seventeen years old," said Coney. Of the fifty-eight members of the Outlaws, Coney said only he and two others decided to abandon the gangster lifestyle.

In the two years after he left the gang, he had been encouraging young people to take a different path than he did. Two weeks later, he was sent to jail for gun possession, drug dealing, and possession. He spent five years in prison. After he was released, he learned that a friend had been murdered. Coney intended to avenge his friend's death but instead of revenge he was introduced to a greater cause. He met Christ and was saved.

Coney joined the H.E.V.N. (Help End Violence Now) Coalition, an organization to help fight against gangs. There he worked as an assistant outreach worker and Hykeim also attended Nassau Community College. His purpose in life, he realized was to serve God by teaching young people who Christ is and helping to end gang violence in the lives of all children. He was looked up to by the young and older people in the community for standing up for such a great cause. He had a voice and he used it for a much better reason in the neighborhood.

He was a pastor in training until his life was cut short at the age of twenty-four by the rage he tried so hard to remove from young people. His funeral was well attended by over three thousand young people throughout the community, in which more than one hundred young people gave their lives to Christ and joined a nearby church as well as the H.E.V.N. organization to continue his work for the Lord.

R.I.P.

Special Thanks To

Pastor Leroy Woodside, since my wife and I have come under your leadership we have learned so much about ourselves by reading the Bible. You have taught us in a practical way how to relate to God. We have become stronger in our walk with Christ. We clearly understand our purpose. We boldly spread the Gospel and we are not ashamed to be representatives of the Kingdom. Thank you for the powerful teaching.

This book is dedicated to:

My father, Bruce Davis Sr. of Union B.C. in Hempstead, New York

Deacon Nathan Murphy of Union B.C. in Hempstead, New York

Deacon Ira Williams of Mt. Olive B.C. in Brooklyn, New York

Deacon Russell Taylor of Greater Saint John Church in Upper Marlboro, Maryland.

Additional Thanks

Thank you, God: I thank God for world peace, humanity, joy, clear vision, clear understanding of the "Word" and your unconditional love for us all. I send a special prayer out for all of the men and women serving this great country.

Church Family: My Pastor Leroy Woodside, Jr., Pastor Yvonne and the entire New York and North Carolina Churches.

Family & Friends: My lovely wife, Tiana and our children, my parents and siblings, aunts, uncles and cousins, Mother-in-law, sister-in-laws and brother-in-law, Ron Ives, Taylor Family, Michelle and Rob, Lorenzo Steele, Adrian Howard, Employees of Jadé, Gina Slater Parker, Tammy Calderon and her family, **Union Baptist Church Family**, Ms. Jackie, Ms. Charlotte, Deacon Johnson of Faith B.C., Class of 91 Uniondale HS, Thorton Family, Tricia Ferrell for putting God first, Hykiem Coney and family, L. Cobbs **(I.O.U.),** James Counts and family, Sandra Smith, Bro. Thomas Owens, Sergio, Mr. Curry, Doug Thomas Jr.

Bruce K. Davis, Jr.

Clergymen: Preachers of Eastern Baptist Association, Rev. Easley and Yvette (1st Lady of Union B.C.)

Rev. Boone, Rev. Parker, Rev. Brown, Rev. Watson, Rev. Elliott, Rev. McDowell for marrying my wife and I, Rev. Tuggle, Rev. Craig Wright, Bishop White, Dr. Rochford, Pastor Melvin Walker **(R.I.P.)**, Bishop Mackey, Min. Seretta McKnight & Bishop Harris.

Other Black Business Leaders: Burt N. and family, Dec. Mackey, Mr. Woody Print, Nathaniel Barnes, Copy Supreme, Copyman, Black Business owners of LI & BK, Gloria Eve Performing Art School, Deacon Butler of Stand Up Ministry, Community Journal, Glickman Photography

Political Leaders and Organizations:

Roosevelt Kiwanis Club, Hempstead NAACP, Roosevelt/Freeport NAACP, Omega Psi Phi Fraternity Inc., Pi Gamma NSU Chapter

The School Districts of Long Island: Roosevelt H.S., Principal, Mr. Humphrey for his tireless efforts to educate the young people, Mrs. Tootle, Mrs. Green of Uniondale H.S., Mr. Stroughn, Ms. Pat Brown, Bro. Keys and family, Mr. Hank Williams of Hempstead H.S., Dr. Lloyd, Supt. of Uniondale H.S., Mr. Potter, Ret. Prin., Mrs. Simmons, Prin. Of Uniondale H.S., Ms. Green and Jeanine Bradley of UHS

Institutions: Norfolk State University, Hampton University and The United States Navy.

Part One

Pastor Money, the Pastor of U2 Can Get Saved Non-Denominational Church, served over seven thousand members. The mega church served people through television, radio and books. U2CGS had well over fifty ministries under one umbrella. This Sunday, Pastor Money was more dynamic and exhilarating than some of the younger clergymen. The grandfather had given a poignant sermon. As he stood with his lavender suit, purple ostrich skin shoes and long gray, curly hairdo; his voice was perfected to touch the depth of the most sinful soul.

He perspired profusely as he moved around on a platform made for a rock star. His jewelry marveled that of a rapper. He glanced from time to time at his well-written papers that lay on a gold podium adorned with ornate floral arrangements along the bottom of the stage. He seemed to pamper himself as he removed the sweat that streamed from his forehead as if he was working out. The musicians followed his every utterance. The sanctuary was in sync with the spirit. Everyone envisioned God appearing and moving through the entire sanctuary during service.

His subject was, "Killing the dreams of our children". He began to preach, "Anyone my age and if you are of Color, knows what it was like when people were trying to kill your dreams, your father's dreams, your children's dreams and anyone who dreamed to have better. What would have become of some of us if some of our dreams would not have come true?" The congregation stared as he continued to preach from his structured sermon. Those that understood yelled out, "AMEN."

The younger members of the church were prudently listening as their Pastor talked passionately about them. Whatever God did for him to receive his message, it was felt. The congregation followed his every word. Pastor Money continued to preach as his voice began to resound louder and louder, "how long did it take before some of you older members of this church realized your purpose in life? Young people, do you know what type of potential you have if you put your best foot forward?" The Pastor went as far as calling the names of some of the celebrities the younger people related to, which only helped draw the teen's attention to his sermon. "Young ladies can be the next Jennifer Hudson, the new Mary J. Bilge or Oprah and our young men; you can be the next Kanye West, Will Smith or Senator

Barack Obama." Everyone turned to one another with a smile and nodded their heads in agreement to what Pastor Money was saying. "Jesus Christ's enemies knew his purpose and the good within him. They set out to kill him before he was born. What our children face today is the same persecution Jesus faced before he was killed at the early age of thirty-three."

Pastor Money noticed he was losing his younger people in great numbers. He needed the help of his older and loyal members but they were more inclined to push traditional church values down the kids' throats. The kids were rebelling and did the very opposite of what they saw being introduced by those before them. How was he going to bridge the gap and make both old and young people in his church realize they were in much need of one another? If his older members did not share their knowledge, it would surely perish and go with them to their graves. His young people were listening to the media, music and internet but not their parents. He wanted to implement a class that could teach the "Word" to his younger members in its raw form. But the class had to be practical.

The sermon was on fire and everyone received the "Word". Pastor Money, from the heart and with conviction then turned to the congregation and asked them for a love donation. "You heard what the Lord has said; now we need all our older members to give a hundred dollars. This love offering will go to building a future for our children. I want our young people to ask your parents to help you each bring twenty dollars, so you can receive your blessing. Pastor Money's for the kids, AMEN." The church got quiet and those that said, "Amen" during the sermon were not as loud this time.

Lucious Bell, in his early thirties, resembled Jamie Fox, the actor, Oscar winner, comedian and musician. He was asked the previous Friday by the pastor to lead the church youth group in a bi-weekly open discussion to find out what young people were thinking and how they felt about certain issues relating to their generation. He contemplated as he headed out the door of his home at 5:45 a.m.

It was autumn. Lucious knew it was that time of year when his wife would drag him up and down the aisles at Roosevelt Field Mall in Garden City. She would look for all the latest trendy winter clothes. Lucious smiled in approval at each outfit, although, just about everything she picked up looked like something she already had in her walk-in closet. Occasionally, he would ask; "What about this? She'd respond to Lucious' questions as she pulled Ebony and Lucky magazines from her Louis Vuitton monogram "Mirage Griet" tote bag, "that was so last season; this is what I am looking for." What was a good husband suppose to do as his wife dragged him from Macy's, Bloomingdale's and Nordstrom's Department stores? He was to give his opinion only when asked, pay the bill and carry the bags.

The weather seemed to sporadically go from cold to hot, rainy to sunny. Luscious as a restaurant owner adjusted part of his daily operation depending on the weather. His soul food restaurant was placed in the middle of a predominately Black and Hispanic community in Hempstead, Long Island. Southern Cuisine was a full service restaurant. He prided himself in knowing his responsibility and task was to remove the stigma of a soul food restaurant. He knew that he had to go against the myth of a hole in the wall greasy, unprofessional, poorly managed place with employees boasting bad attitudes. His job was far from easy, although a few reality T.V. shows appeared to make it look like a walk in the park. He knew almost any average African-American with a southern background could cook the product he was offering but could they deliver the product the same as a five star restaurant delivered their food to their guests?

Lucious set out to offer his community something it did not have as an amenity to living in his town; a classy, clean, professional place with great tasting soul food served to them on a silver platter and their choice of wine served to them in a glass. They would be able to wipe their mouths with a linen napkin and listen to gospel and jazz music as they rub shoulders with politicians, preachers and celebrities. When Lucious chose his location, he did not factor the amount of resources he would spend on educating an entire community. His full service restaurant was surrounded by take-out Chinese, Spanish Bodegas and Jamaican restaurants. Although the customers loved the crystal glasses, some were only willing to pay for Styrofoam cups.

Lucious was half asleep as he drove on the empty streets less then five miles from his home to the restaurant. As he cruised toward the restaurant, he saw lights flashing and moments later he noticed cop cars coming from every direction. They were after someone and they did not want whomever it was to know they were moving in. He parked his Ford Explorer, which was the company truck, in front of the restaurant and glanced down the street to see all the action that was happening a block away.

The streets were full of debris as the sun slowly began to appear. The night crawlers moved in the direction of the cop cars instead of going into their hidings, as they would normally do as darkness turned to light. The birds chirped as a few stragglers sluggishly prowled the sidewalk. Lucious reached down to pick up a bundle of local newspapers dropped in front of his restaurant door, locked the door behind himself and quickly dropped the bundle down on the hard wooden floor as he went to turn off the alarm. He turned on the all the televisions to the local news channel and walked through the restaurant. He knew he had less then a half an hour of peace and serenity, if it was possible, with all that was going on a block away before his morning cooks would arrive to start preparing to open his doors at eight.

Lucious began to make coffee as his attention was captured by the television. The news reporter was reporting two young Black teenagers being placed in the back of a cop car. He hurried to turn the television volume up as he walked over to pick up the stack of newspapers from the floor. He stared out the door of the restaurant to see cop cars silently rushing up the street and a small crowd circling around ten cop cars with lights flashing from each of their vehicles. He turned back to the television only to comprehend what was taking place was happening up the street from his business. The local news reporter continued to commentate. Her bias description practically indicted the two teenagers for murder.

Her stoic appearance was contrary to the situation. The cameraman focused on the reporter but the viewers could not help but notice the chaos occurring behind the reporter. The policemen and women were busy blocking the streets off from ongoing traffic, redirecting the city buses and other vehicles as the street began to build up with onlookers heading off to work. The red headed, amateur reporter was Rebecca Stanton. She fingered through her frizzy hair and said, "Although, the crime rate has dropped in Nassau County these murders that were unfolded by the Nassau Police Department in a year long undercover operation, involved the deaths of over fifty rival gang members. The murders allegedly committed by these heartless gangsters were said to occur not just in Long Island but also as far south as Durham, North Carolina. The chief of Police, who will give a press conference at ten o'clock this morning, told me; one of these young men has a criminal background that began as early as nine years old. The chief informed me that the operation came to a close when the undercover officer who worked his way inside of one these gangs saw first hand the violent life style these gang members lived. The Chief of Nassau County also told me, the identity of the undercover officer is not being released due to the severity of this case. But the officer was said to have resigned from the force after witnessing the amount of blood shed in this year long investigation. We have been following this report carefully. A reliable source told Channel 20, the undercover officer, was hired in 2006 and was practically a rookie. He was on the force for less than two years and because of his gang affiliation prior to joining the police force, he was able to go further than any other law enforcement officer has ever gone, until it all came to a deadly end. Our source said the officer in question feared his life and his family's lives.

Channel 20 reported that last night there was a gang war, which took place at about six in the evening on these very same streets. After the fatal shooting stopped, six gang members under the age of eighteen had died and six others were sent to Nassau Medical Center in East Meadow with life threatening injuries. After the mayhem, the suspects rallied other gang members and allegedly came back to this block to revenge the deaths of their gang members." The reporter went on to close her report by saying, "There hasn't been a case like this in the state of New York since the FBI investigated the connection between the Italian mob and several deaths that left bodies laid out in pools of blood in the 80's. But unlike in that case it appears that these killers will be brought to justice. This is Rebecca Stanton, Channel 20, reporting live from Hempstead." As the reporter wrapped up her report, bystanders obnoxiously jumped in front of the camera; screaming out, "Welcome to Iraq. We're at war."

The phone rang at the same time Lucious' two cooks were unlocking the front door. "Thank you for calling Southern Cuisine, this is Lucious speaking, how may I serve you?" Lucious delivered the telephone greeting without thought. He mouthed the words "Good Morning" and used hand gestures to communicate to his cooks as he continued talking to his wife. "I'm fine, Baby." Lucious said to his wife who called concerned. He tried to hold more than one conversation and not let his wife know he was paying half attention to her while she feared for his life. "I know, dear." One of the cooks picked up the local newspaper to quietly show Lucious the incident that had happen yesterday, regarding the gang. The front page read, GANG KILLERS. "Yes Honey, I heard every word you've said." Lucious said to Sarah as he turned the page. His mouth dropped when he looked at fifty pictures of young Black men. Under each picture, the Long Island newspaper stated their names, date of birth and date of death. But Lucious became even more speechless when he notice these young men were all killed in the last twelve months; and lived between New York and North Carolina. *I can't believe this.* Lucious thought to himself. Lucious eyes traveled from one Black face to the next on the paper. *The first thing that came to his mind was the Black serial killer in Atlanta, Georgia who kidnapped and killed all those Black children in the 80's. Why?*

Lucious was distracted by his thoughts as he tried to continue the conversation with Sarah, he struggled to find words. "I'm sorry but from what this reporter is saying on T.V., the bodies they found last night were found up the street from the restaurant, somewhere on Main Street." Pointing to the street, Lucious directed the cook. He asked his cook what was going on in front of the restaurant. "Boss man, they've blocked off the street in front of the restaurant." The cook, who was old enough to be Lucious' father yelled from the door with his southern accent. "Honey, I have to go. These people are about to mess me up." Before his wife could ask another question, Lucious abruptly hung up the phone and was in front of the building looking for answers.

During the time Lucious and his wife were courting, they worked diligently together on grants helping to bring funds for youth programs to their church. They both graduated from a Historically Black College. Lucious studied political science and Sarah studied to become an educator. They enjoyed working with children but Lucious found himself entranced with his business ventures. Sarah resembled Jada Pinkett Smith. Her petite frame showed off her curves and Lucious loved her long thick hair. He thought she was the most beautiful woman he knew. In every area Lucious lacked, Sarah exceeded. Lucious was in a "people" business and Sarah had an abundance of personal friends.

Lucious always jokingly told his wife he was not in fear of some of her friends filling her head with problems. If they were not on the prowl looking for single men, they were trying to ruin the homes with one in it. They were not influential in his wife's life because she could look at her own and tell she had it much better than the friends she kept. But the "friends in her head" were special. Lucious defined a friend in his wife's head as: women, his wife does not know personally but if she ever met them, she surely would make them her friend; a woman that another woman admires. Sarah's friends in her head were Wendy Williams; (New York Radio Host), Sarah Jessica Parker (Actress/Fashionista), Oprah Winfrey (Talk Show Host) and Kimora Lee Simmons (founder of Baby Phat & author of

Fabulosity). Whatever these celebrity women said or wore dictated his home. And whenever these women held local events, Sarah was certain to be there.

Lucious understood who Christ was but some how wondered if he was serving his purpose in life. It was not until after he graduated from college and lived in another state, that he found Christ and learned what it took to fight the adversaries. He found Christ, yet he was not a spiritual man but a man who religiously attended church. The question that stuck deep in his mind was *if a child's parents accepted nothing but excellence, what would a child become?* He didn't do so badly in life but not much was expected of him other than to honestly work for a living. But Lucious knew the areas he was weak in and he set out to surround himself with those who could help build his character.

That Friday on a bitter cold afternoon, Pastor Money called a meeting with Lucious and the deacon board. It was fresh on all their minds the unpleasant incident that had taken place earlier in the week. Just as the community was becoming immune to the deaths and the fatal occurrences involving gangs they could not ignore the situation that rocked the town. Pastor Money was not about to let this become old news over night as much as his older members blamed the younger generation for their own self destruction. He wanted to form a class to help bridge the gap between the young people in the church and the rest of the congregation. The church membership had an average age of sixty-five years of age. "Brother Bell, I have one requirement of you." As the pastor continued to talk, Lucious was busy asking himself questions in his head. The questions began to show on his face, as did on the faces of the board members. The pastor stopped talking and began to answer questions without him asking. Pastor Money said, "I have asked Lucious to lead this class because he seems to have the true understanding of our young people." "We," as he looked in the eyes of the others sitting at the table, "are too old to get our young people to open up. I want this class to take place every other week on Friday nights; but not in place of Wednesday night bible study. I want this class to be applicable to these young people. The Bible will back up every subject discussed. However, this is only for the high school youngsters." The pastor looked excited about this new class but the older board members seemed to have a different vision. Their bodies were there but their minds could not relate and in silence they disagreed until shown differently.

Bruce K. Davis, Jr.

Roman 8:27 "Now He (God) who searches the hearts knows what the mind of the Spirit is, because He makes intercession for the saints according to the will of God."
1 Corinthians 2:11, John 16:13

The pastor looked around the table with the biggest grin on his face and said, "I would like to call this class, Rap Session. That sounds catchy and the young people enjoy rap music. I want our young people to prepare themselves for the coming of the Lord. The music, our young people are listening to is destroying our youth. When our Lord and Savior Jesus Christ come again, only those that profess He is Lord will live." "AMEN," Everyone boastfully said as they looked at one another with a sign of approval.

Lucious was glad Pastor Money was implementing a new ministry for the young people but he did not think he was the right person to lead this class. Before the pastor ended the meeting with a prayer, he quickly asked as they held hands, "does anyone have any questions?"

Lucious wanted to yell out to everyone sitting in this meeting but remaining silent, *"What does rapture mean, again?"* The Pastor looked around the table, as if he was reading each and every facial expression. "Brother Bell, this will be announced and placed in this week's bulletin. I want to see this up and running by the first of the month." He gave prayer. Everyone slowly walked out of the conference room but Lucious waited for the right moment to talk with the pastor and the chairman of the Deacon Board. He had doubts and questions. He did not doubt his pastor but himself and his capabilities to teach anything of the bible.

The board had confidence in Lucious, but Lucious had other things to consider before he took on this type of challenge. He spent much of his time working in his business and his new marriage was still hitting a few bumps. *"My professional life is struggling and my marriage is still on trial,"* he thought to himself. If he had to endure another thing in life he would be asking one of the ministers in the church for counseling.

Part Two

While the Pastor was busy walking and talking with the board members, the Chairman of the Deacon Board pulled Lucious over to the side and gave him a few words. He was always known as the most spiritual man in the church and in his "hay day" he would stand up against any group in the church he felt was not of the "**Word**". He knew the Bible back and forth but was still very down to earth and he chose his battles very carefully since he was always placed in the middle of church politics.

He had a way of getting you to understand when you were wrong by first asking you what you thought, then reciting a scripture off the top of his head; easily going to it with you and then telling you what he thought about the matter. He was great at leaving you with a thought and answer but room for you to make your own discussions. Lucious guessed Deacon Taylor had figured the person should be capable of finding the answer on their own.

"Brother Bell," Deacon Taylor whispered to catch Lucious' attention, "You may feel like you are not ready to lead this group of young people but you are. You may not know the bible as well as you should, but God knows your heart. You have been called to teach but while you are teaching, you are being taught." Deacon Taylor paused as he ministered to Lucious.

"You, young people, are looking for leadership and guidance. All the great Kings of Africa and the awesome Leaders of the Civil Rights Era (my time) were assassinated, only to destroy peace. The National Leaders today are not being assassinated but are slowly being ruined by the media and other sources by destroying their character. They assassinate their characters and point out their flaws, so the people who are being led by them will have heavy doubt. They just flat out crucified Jesus." Deacon Taylor paused for a second.

"Let's use Bill Cosby for example. He spoke out. He wanted change in the lower economic community. He felt the lower class African-Americans was not holding their end of the deal. He wanted to protest against drug dealers, pregnant teens, deadbeat dads, and hate-filled rap music that celebrated violence; but after they finished assassinating Bill Cosby's character, America quickly forgot he was a "Huxtable" and all he had done to help the Black community. By the time they finished with #1 dad figure in America, he was treated like a deadbeat dad and had gone into hiding." Deacon paused another second, to catch his breath but to see if his young listener understood the words and his message. "Granted the problems of our communities are not 100% our fault. There are some evil people with there hands in the pot. They are busy stirring up all sorts of chaos and hell. But I believe Mr. Cosby was trying to say, we are allowing this to happen to ourselves. He probably is wondering why he opened his mouth in the first place. But children have to realize, the Bible says in

Romans 3:10 as it is written; there is no one righteous, not even one. Roman 3:23 says, for all has sinned and fall short of the glory of God.

The other board members noticed Deacon Taylor had young Lucious trapped and the young leader was being pumped of knowledge. If he made it pasted the old wise man then he would be okay but if he never showed up for the class, then they knew he was not ready. Deacon Taylor continued speaking, "We can not look to man, to be our savior and for all the answers because no one man has all the answers. It takes hundreds of men and women to sit in congress or the senate to come up with one law but it takes one God to make a law. Children have to know for sure, the power they hold. They have to be their own leader and let God order their steps and they have to do less talking and more listening." If that was not enough for Lucious to take in, what Deacon Taylor said next only caused Lucious to walk away with a mighty headache all the knowledge he received from this one person.

"The Truth of the Matter is: Our lives are predestined. Everything that happens in your life has already been set in stone but when you figure out your purpose in life, you'll set out for greatness. There are two journeys in all of our lives; first finding your purpose and then fulfilling it. You will stop thinking about yourself at that point and set out to make a difference in the lives of others. But in order for you to see your purpose, God is going to take you through a series of tests; some small but some not so small. You must hold on tightly because when you come out of the darkness, the light will be blinding; and at that point you will understand why you have been placed here. You'll see that some things are out of Lucious' control; and that which is in your control you'll give it your best. God has something in store for you that is going to blow your mind. Take a chance. You're in business; you know what it is like to take chances."

The message was powerful. It sunk in to Lucious mind. "Son, there are a few things I can help you understand.

1. You must be prepared and study because young people can eat the best Christian up, when you are not sure what the **Word** says and what man says.
2. If you want the truth seek God but children are God's innocence, children do not know how to lie with a straight face.
3. In this program, you will be able to judge your success by your own growth, when you grow those around you will grow with you.
4. Follow your heart and not your mind. The **Word** will come through your heart and that is what young people will listen to.
5. Each week have a real life subject that you can back up with scripture.
6. Truth is not debatable. If you back up what you are saying with what the bible says, then they cannot debate the bible. (Don't allow them to try.)

Deacon Taylor continued schooling Lucious, "I want you to go home and pray about what I talked about. If this is what God has for you then he will confirm his plan for your life. When that happens you will know it is an established word. Consider what I've just said as the first confirmation to what God has for you to do." Lucious was beyond asking any questions, he felt like he was beat down and had lost a fight to an eighty year old man in a wheel chair, who could barely breathe. He was looking at Deacon Taylor as if he was confirming to himself that this task was hard and God could probably use another voice on the choir. "I know you are busy in your restaurant business, so is this going to conflict with your business on Friday nights?" Deacon Taylor asked. This was the chance for Lucious to get out of it by playing like he was the busiest man on earth but he liked a good challenge; and would like to study the Bible.

For once in his life he was making time for bible study but he was not sure about teaching young people on a subject he was unclear of. He wondered why the Pastor did not place him in charge of the business ministry. Deacon Taylor did not want to leave him without helping him gain his confidence. "Brother Bell," Deacon Taylor said, "since I usually eat at your restaurant just about every other day, how about you and I sit down once a week at your restaurant during your slowest time? We can go over the topic you plan to discuss with the young people and how it relates to the bible. I want you to be clear about what you are teaching the young people." Lucious smiled even bigger when the Deacon said, "I will sit in this rap session class, with you. I will make sure that you and I are the only two oldest people in this class, that way our young people can open up and freely speak. I will not say a word but I will be there as the guy who backs up the rap artist and repeats every word. Almost like your back up singer." Lucious was impressed because for the Chairman of the Deacon Board and a person old enough to be his grandfather, it told Lucious; he really wanted this for the young people.

Deacon Taylor shook Lucious' hand. He pulled him in and gave a grandfatherly bear hug from his wheelchair. As Lucious headed for the door, Deacon Taylor called out his name, "Brother Bell." Lucious stopped and turned in Deacon Taylor's direction. "The first thing I would like you to do for an old man is look up the word, "Rapture" and read what the bible says about it or if it says anything at all?" Lucious took it as his first homework assignment.

Part Three

An ominous cloud showed signs of rain. As Lucious walked out of the church he realized the temperature had dropped. The previous days were warm but today felt like as if he needed to pull out his winter coat. One of the young people who is a member of the church quickly approached him about a matter that seemed to be pressing. As Lucious stood by his Ford Explorer with his keys dangling from his hand, ready to leap into his vehicle to escape the chilling cold air; all the while looking toward the sky at the dark clouds hovering over them. Aaron Jordan, the son of one of the trustees in the church casually walked up to Lucious. His mother was not far away. She was in the meeting with Lucious, the Pastor and other board members. "Lucious, you have a minute?" asked Aaron. He was well spoken but when he was around his peers his English grammar was easily replaced with Black vernacular. Aaron was a young teenager with a bright future ahead of him. He did not carry any signs of a troubled teen but a typical teen bound to get into trouble. He knew how to speak and what to say around church members but away from home and church he was a part time thug. Aaron's mother had stopped fighting her son about his breads in his hair. Aaron weighed a buck and a half. His pants were always worn five times his size and constantly falling off his waist. The black hooded sweated that swallowed his frail body and covered the majority of his face was triple the size a person his normal size should wear. He tried harder to look like one of the thousands of children walking in the neighborhood rather than standing out as handsome as his mother saw him to be.

Lucious was torn; he didn't mind being called by his first name, but he knew if he had any children, he would want to train his children to call people of age Mister or Ms. He was at that age in his life where he had to face the **_Truth of the Matter_** is: he was getting older. He suddenly thought one way to hold on to his youth would be to work on a first name basis with the youth.

"Yeah... What's up Aaron?" Lucious knew by the tone of Aaron's groggy voice, his body language and by the fact that his blood shot eyes faced the ground. From Aaron's hesitation and his unexpected shyness Lucious braced himself for the worst. Aaron was known as the class clown; usually very upbeat, making jokes and looking for attention.

He reached out his hand and as Lucious leaned in to shake his hand. Aaron's youthful hand shake began with a series of slaps and finger pointing that seemed more like thumb wrestling than hand shaking. The hand shake alone told Lucious he was out of touch. "Is my mom's still inside the church?" Aaron asked. Lucious could see he did not know where to begin but if he wanted to say something, he did not have much time before their conversation would be interrupted. "I have a small problem and I need your help with this problem." Aaron said as he slurred his words. Lucious could only imagine the worst, as he tried to look into Aaron's wondering red eyes, thinking it could not be that bad. This kid is the son of one of the trustees in the church, he comes from a good church home and he is considered one of the community's star kids. He was a leader amongst his peers. "I'm going to make it short," Aaron began to say. "You heard on the news about all those cats that were killed this past week?" Aaron looked at Lucious. Lucious looked at Aaron waiting for his point. "Yeah! It's sparked some craziness but not just around here but it's sweeping all the hoods. I'm talking about 'beef' between people in East Coast, West Coast, Mid West, and the Dirty South. If you know what I'm sayin? Lucious was confused. "No, Aaron. I don't have a clue about what you are saying. Aaron began to show his rage. His eyes pierced through Lucious' soul. Aaron boyish posture began to erect. His hands balled into a powerful fist. He began to show his other side by his innocence and charismatic demeanor quickly changing before Lucious eyes. Lucious did not know this other person who lived within Aaron. Aaron stood tall in front of Lucious as an angry man.

"So, Aaron, what seem to be the problem?" Lucious quickly asked, hoping he could be some help but really wanting to get out of the cold. Aaron noticed Lucious began to grow impatience. He had stopped stuttering and threw it out there. "This Spanish kid, who lives down the block from me, we had some problems. We fought yesterday and now it has escalated into something big."

Lucious tried to understand everything he was being told by Aaron, while thinking to himself, *Okay, two young men having a fight.* He had had a fight or two in high school but today these young people are carrying guns and knives but Aaron was not the type. *Maybe, Aaron is telling me he is afraid. He is not telling me something.* Aaron stood there looking at the ground in silence as though Lucious was supposed to guess the rest of his issue.

"Aaron, if you don't tell me what is going on, I can't help you. Tell me what's up; we can come up with a solution. And what does any of this have to do with the Gangs that have been killing each other, on the news?" Aaron looked at Lucious dead in the eyes and began to tell him the story but he was talking so fast, he began to stutter, again. "See, this Spanish kid who lives down the block from me belongs to this gang.

Lucious' mind started to race. He thought he had a problem with some kid that happened to be in a gang. If he had to fight one gang member, he would have to fight the entire gang.' "Aaron, what we can do is talk to your mom and then bring this to the school's attention before someone really gets hurt." Aaron was silent for a second. He whispered in a frustrated under-tone. "When things pop off, his gang will not be the only problem. My people will be ready to get at 'dem'." Lucious looked at Aaron both shocked and confused. "Holding your peace doesn't make you weak," Lucious mentioned not realizing he was quoting the Bible.

Roman 12:19 "Dearly beloved, avenge not yourselves, but rather give place unto wrath: for it is written, Vengeance is mine, I will repay, saith the Lord."

Lucious, although very intelligent had just caught on. He stopped asking questions and as all the pieces to the puzzle began to come together. "Aaron, are you involved in a gang? Are you a gang member?" His silence answered Lucious' question. Lucious suddenly realized Aaron's attire represented more than just a fashion statement. His red fitted baseball cap and his red sneakers; they all made sense now. Before Lucious could say another word Aaron's mother walked over. It was cold but not freezing enough for Trustee Jordan to pull her fur collection out from storage. The same makeup artist who probably painted Tammy Faye Baker's face and the hair stylist who worked on Diana Ross's hair for the past two decades did her eyelashes. "Hello Brother Lucious, I see my son has caught your ear." Her mouth moved broadly to articulate each word she pronounced with precision. Two of Aaron's friends joined them, shoes...shirts...hats...Lucious had never paid it much attention before, but now he couldn't help but notice. Aaron's mother continued, "I'm sure the young people in our church will appreciate this new Rap Session Ministry." "Rap session...let me find out?" Aaron and his friends laughed. "What is that about?" "Brother Bell is going to head a class for young people, where you all will be able to discuss real issues relating to you; and it's called 'The Rap Session'.

How does that sound?" Trustee Jordan's doubts were slightly eased when she saw her son's friend's reaction. Lucious continued to observe Aaron as he kept his composure, remained silent and said few words in his mother's presence. Questions from the three boys started flying. "Do you have to go to this church to be a part of this?" "Yeah, can we bring friends?" "Is this like boring bible study?" "Is this class for the all the kids in the church or just us?" "Will our parents be there?" "Is there going to be food?" Lucious had his own questions, but had few answers. He glanced at Trustee Jordan, for help. "We are still figuring everything out, but don't worry, the church has your best interest at heart." Spoken like a true politician with no answer to the question. "We will answer all of those questions when they make the announcement," Lucious replied.

As Aaron and his friends ran to catch up with some girls, Lucious quickly unlocked the doors of his truck, indicating to Trustee Jordon he was in a rush to get back to the restaurant. Before he was held up another minute, he had already placed one foot into his vehicle. Meanwhile, Trustee Jordon had slipped into her 500 series Mercedes sitting beside Lucious' company truck. "Lucious!" Aaron shouted from a distance. "I mean Mr. ... umm Brother Bell" Aaron felt his mother's stare. "Can I come by the restaurant and talk to you about a job?" Lucious saw that as a great idea. He smiled at Aaron before leaping into his truck. Trustee Jordan was happy her son had someone like Lucious to look up to in the church. Her husband passed away from lung cancer a few years earlier; and she was trying her best to be a mother and a father to her only child. Lucious briefly sat still in his vehicle as Deacon Taylor came to mind. He felt Aaron's fear. He was caught between being a boy and proving to his friends, he was a man.

Wow! He had just received his second confirmation. God was telling Lucious, *Young people need an outlet and a clear understanding of who God is and how it all applied to their everyday lives.* Lucious saw that God was working fast; he hadn't even left the parking lot of the church. Lucious began to think harder as the rain suddenly hit his truck.

Part Four

It had been a long day and Lucious was exhausted. He was thankful because his home was just minutes away. The restaurant, his home, and the church were all minutes from one another. Even the movie theater, Starbucks and the mall were within walking distance. He never had to leave his Long Island neighborhood but he and his wife often had date night in New York City and although it was nearly an hour away, Lucious sometimes felt claustrophobic by remaining in the same environment.

It was common for him and his wife to travel to Manhattan to see a Broadway play, and on occasionally spent the night in the city. Lucious was romantic and very much in love. He and his wife would book weekend trips just for a quick break from reality. They wanted to break away from having a boring routine in such an early marriage. They tried spicing up the relationship by doing little things that required more time and precise planning rather then money. He always felt trapped and in a bubble when everything in their lives was at such a short distance in their small tight-knit community. But the business demanded much of Lucious' time and soon he found himself trapped more and more in the bubble he tried so hard to (break free) from. In Lucious' bubble he traveled to three destinations, church, home and the restaurant. After a while the only sizzle in his life is from the plates coming out of the restaurant kitchen.

From this, arguments with Sarah began to get intense as they spent less and less time with each other. Lucious began struggling financially with his business and much of the stress affected their relationship. The more he threw himself into the business, the more he expected his wife to understand. He felt he could not do as much as he did before and used the business as his excuse, although he knew he could always "think outside the box" and find creative ways of spending time with his wife.

Instead of ordering room service from an exquisite menu, in an elaborate hotel or purchasing tickets to the latest Broadway play; they could travel to a vineyard on Long Island and have lunch. Instead of traveling to the Caribbean for an extended weekend, they could drive to the Hamptons on Long Island. He could always find ways to cut costs, but how could he find the time? Lucious realized his business and his relationship would cost him one way or another. He often thought of his parents' relationship. They worked themselves into the ground before they realized they had to find time for each other. For his parents, spending quality time with each other became a challenge instead of a luxury. Lucious father was constantly away on business. After living so many years without his presence and finding out he had another family elsewhere, Lucious mother filed for divorce. He didn't want that to happen to him and Sarah.

"Sarah, I'm home." He walked through the door with a small plate he put together for dinner and a flower from the restaurants weekly delivery. They had not seen much of each other lately. He was working long hours in the restaurant and she was busy preparing her students for state exams.

Lucious heard movement in the bathroom as he headed to the kitchen. He prepared their plates and placed the flower in a vase. Lately, Sarah had become particularly moody. He thought she might find the lily a romantic touch.

1 Corinthians 13:11 "When I was a boy, I spoke as a boy, I understood as a boy, I thought as a boy; but when I became a man, I put away boyish ways.

"How was your day, babe?" She asked. "Great, how was your day with those bad kids you teach?" She forced a half smile onto her face. "My kids are not bad; they just have a few issues. All they need is for their fathers to step up and be men." He remained silent Lucious did not know where the conversation was going and nor did he wish to know.

He quickly began saying grace. "Let us pray. Thank you, God. Please bless this food and the hands that prepared it. May others receive the same nourishment, Amen." Lucious was already jumping into the banana pudding when he noticed that Sarah had barely touched her food before she returned to the bathroom. "Are you okay, babe?"

Lucious knocked on the bathroom door. "Sarah?" "What" "Are you okay? Are you sick? Do you need me to get you something?" Silence. She walked out of the bathroom pushing past Lucious and headed back into the dining room. "Why are you so impatient with children? If you were in my shoes and worked with some of these kids you would find they are crying out for help but men like you are too busy and caught up with your careers, hobbies, toys and sports that you can't see the big picture." Lucious thought if, *she gave me a chance I could tell her about the new youth ministry.* "Sarah.' He called but she kept rambling. "Sarah.' He called the second time. She excused herself and ran back to the bathroom. Lucious walked back over to the bathroom door as he heard her letting go what little she ate.

"Sarah. Today, I was in a meeting with Pastor Money. He wants me to help with a youth group at the church. I'm excited and Aaron and his boys are too." She lifted her head out from the toilet, looked over at Lucious as to say who is Aaron? "Trustee Jordan's son, the kid in your high school, you know?" He said as he gently rubbed her back. "Please excuse me." Sarah impolitely asked and then shut the door in her husband's face.

Lucious continued through the door. "I saw them, Aaron and his boys, right after we got out of the meeting with Pastor Money. I don't know where to begin and I don't want to let these kids down. I was wondering…" The door opened slowly to the bathroom. She looked him in the eyes and without another delay said, "I'm happy that you are working with the young people, again. I'm glad you've found time for something other than yourself and that business of yours. You and I used to love working with children and we had time for one another. Do you remember? Now you have become consumed with work. You need to learn how to balance your life and I think this new thing at church will help you understand what you've lost…patience. You are going to need a lot of that soon." Lucious just stood there, *what does she mean, I need patience,* he asked himself. "We need to talk," said Sarah.

They peacefully sat at the table. Lucious had questioned what was bothering her for weeks. He had been trying to figure her out but she had been very uptight. She had been distant and very moody but Lucious was about to fix the problem; maybe taking her out, spending some time with his wife would help.

Lucious sat next to her, held her hands, and looked into her big brown eyes. "What's wrong, Baby?" He asked in concern for her but more so for himself. "I know what you are dealing with and it's my fault. I have made you unhappy and yes, I have consumed myself with the business. Whatever you want it's yours and from now on, I will make time for us." As tears began to roll down her face, he started to think. He knew breaking rule #1 as a married man would cost him big time. *Never admit you're wrong,* he thought to himself as he punished himself in his head. He could not take anymore. "Whatever you are facing, we can face it together. We are married and if you are not happy, then I'm not happy. Are you going to tell me what you are dealing with?" He asked with force.

Colossians 3:25 *"But he who does wrong will be repaid for what he has done, and there is no partially."*

Just as Sarah took a deep breath, the phone rang. They both tried ignoring it until the voice came piercing through the answering machine. "Hello, Lucious, if you are home I need to talk to you." Aaron was so nervous; he continued to talk into the answering machine. "The weekend is here but I still have to deal with that problem at the school. I got your number from the church directory; I hope its okay that I am calling you at home instead of at the restaurant. Oh yeah! Don't call my house because I don't want my Moms' knowing and can we leave Mrs. Bell out of this because she is my teacher; and I know if she... Well you understand." His wife squeezed his hand, as they continued to look at the answering machine Aaron rambled as if he was talking to a person on the other end. Suddenly Sarah blurted out "I'm pregnant."

Part Five

Sarah sat looking for some expression on his face. Then, she picked the phone up, "Hi Aaron; hold on for Lucious." Lucious' mouth was left hanging wide open as Sarah handed him the phone before walking to the bedroom.

"What's up Aaron?" A sigh of relief came through the phone as Aaron tried to sum up the story from which he left off earlier in the day. "Aaron, I'm listening but can we talk about this another time?" Obviously, what he had to say could not wait because Aaron quickly said, "Nah." Aaron quickly interjected before Lucious could get off the phone, "Word around the way is, the Spanish kid and his crew is planning action against me on Monday. My people were already around my way and I know something is gonna pop off. If he comes for me, he's getting served." A long pause came from Lucious, "Mr. Bell did you just hear what I said? It's gon' down." Lucious finally spoke, "Yes, I heard you." Lucious tried calming Aaron down but while he realized the seriousness of the situation he couldn't help thinking about what Sarah had just told him.

"Being brave is one thing. Being stupid is another. A brave man doesn't look for trouble. He knows when to fight. Aaron, let me handle everything. Give me your cell number and I'll have an answer for you first thing in the morning. I do not feel comfortable about leaving your mom out of the loop, so I have to sleep and pray on all this and then get back at you."

He could not hang the phone up fast enough before running to Sarah to ask a million questions. He still wanted to finish where they left off before Aaron's phone call. "Sarah, when were you going to tell me? How long have you known. Now, I understand." Lucious was rambling, but determined to get the information out of her. He could not figure out the answers to other people's problems without first placing the pieces together in his own life.

They were married for less than a year. The discussion on having children was never clear. They have talked about Sarah first, finishing her master degree and the business being financially stable before having any children. But this plan would cause them to hold off from having any children for two, maybe three years. Sarah shouted loud and clear, her intentions to have children. The reason for her concentrating on her master degree was to keep busy while her husband worked fifteen hours days building up a business. Lucious knew Sarah was always ready for motherhood. Being a parent was something they both wanted but timing was everything to Lucious. *It was not the right time*, thought Lucious. He looked confused rather then happy. His thoughts were racing through his head. He was speechless. Sarah however, was waiting for a response. She was hoping for a different reaction from the father of her unborn child. But his silence infuriated her.

"Wow!" He said shockingly. A big grin covered his face and without another word, he grabbed his wife and tightly hugged her. Jokingly, scared of harming his child, he gently pushes Sarah's body away from his.

"Are you happy?" She asked as she studied his reaction. Sarah wondered if Lucious was really happy or if he was worried about the timing. In reality it was both. Lucious was always talking about the restaurant. He was so consumed with the business. He desperately wanted their lives to be situated before they began a family but Sarah was ready. She was elated, which only made him overjoyed. With everything happening in one day, all at once, he tried to understand God's plan for his life.

Lucious never had to really worry about anyone other than himself. He was married and they needed one another but it was not the same. *A child would come into this world and need my undivided attention*, is all he could think of. "The children in the church are going to need me. My wife needs me." For the first time, he felt needed but it felt scary to be needed by so many. This, to him, was different from those adult friends, family and employees that needed him at any point of his life.

That night Lucious and his wife talked all night about the baby. "What if," was all they could ask? "What if the baby is a girl?" Sarah asked Lucious. "What if the baby is a boy?" Lucious asked. "It does not matter to me, whether we have a girl or a boy. I'd rather a healthy child more then anything." "Would you like to know if we were having a boy or girl?" Sarah was patient. She wanted to be surprised, but she would let Lucious decide whether they would learn the sex of the baby. Lucious placed his head down as he attempted to explain his irrational thinking, "I would rather wait. I believe it will be the most anticipated thing to ever have happen in my life. It's like reading a novel and not being able to get to the end fast enough. I have always had a plan for my life, when it came to my career, my wife and my whole life. This time I want to revel in the anticipation and the surprise. Some things people should wait for, so they can enjoy the surprises in life, see the outcome, see God's miracle, together." Lucious lifted his head and although Sarah spoke no words, her tears said it all.

With all the excitement, they had to bring themselves back to Aaron's problem before the lights were out. Sarah said, "first thing in the morning, I will call my principal at home, making him aware of this situation. We need to put light on this as a whole because it is affecting the entire school and a Band-Aid is not going to cover bullet holes. They have their hands full. Our school is not the only school on stand by. Something is about to happen, something real big. I will see if he will call an assembly with all the alleged gang members in the high school. I thought we knew them all until you find out a kid like Aaron is a part of a gang. They have to stop ignoring this growing problem. We've begun to see signs in the neighborhood a while ago but I think they are waiting for something to happen before they can face the obvious. I will make sure they are not singling out these two young men but try to tackle and face this gang related issue." Lucious quickly tried to ask a question off the subject not realizing she was silently praying. "My bad," he said in a quiet apology.

"Sarah, you study the Bible more than me and come from a Parochial school, so what does the bible say about Rapture?" She was happy about the question because she was not used to Lucious really studying the Bible. She tried to get him into a study habit but realized he had to be ready.

"The Bible doesn't really use the word rapture, but in biblical terms it refers to the 'end of times'. When the bible talks about Jesus' second coming, people call this the rapture. There are actually quite a few scriptures that talk about Jesus' return, would you like me to help you look it up in the Bible?" Lucious quietly said "yes." Lucious was always impressed by how well his wife knew the Bible. She loved to learn and teach.

Sarah rolled over and fell fast asleep. Lucious glanced over at her to ask a question, only to hear her softly purring in her sleep. Lucious whispers, "Just great but what about Aaron's mother? He certainly won't trust confiding in me again," as he gaze upon the mother of his child. He wanted to help the situation not make it worst. Lucious had to ask himself, *if he was my son what would I do if someone gave me this information?* Lucious had to pray because the first thing that came to his mind would send him into a fire, far from Heaven. "I will call the Pastor and let him tell Aaron's mother. He understands counseling and handling all these sorts of problems."

As soon as his eyes got heavy, Lucious realized he just received his third confirmation. It was a revelation. Instead, of passing the responsibility to someone else, he decided … to lead. He'd figured, he made decisions any other time, why pass the buck? "Now, follow your heart and lean not on your own understanding," Deacon Taylor just finished telling him yesterday. Lucious' prayer was not as short as his wife's because he had a lot to talk to God about. There were things happening he did not understand and he knew having a good conversation with God would give him what he needed to go forward. He kneeled down on the opposite side of the bed from his wife and quietly began to speak to God. "Thank you for this gift, forgive me for my selfish ways and bless my wife, our unborn child, Aaron and my wife's students who cry in the dark and myself for what you have surely called me to do. Help me to understand what you have me to do with Aaron and his situation. Give me understanding and direction. Allow these young people to see God as you have me to lead them in the right direction. Please give my relationship with my wife strength and help us to come together as a married couple to make a difference in the lives of your people. Continue to show me how to love my wife and show her how to love me. Bless our home. Bless Aaron. Amen." Lucious silently crawled into the bed beside Sarah. His body from head to toe followed the curves and the way she laid in the bed. He connected his body to hers, as a spoon connects to another spoon. Sarah lay motionless. She closed her eyes after listening to Lucious prayer, in peace.

Part Six

A couple of weeks hurried by and Deacon Taylor has been meeting Lucious at his restaurant regularly. This Friday will be the first class session. Lucious rushed over to Deacon Taylor's table in the restaurant, hoping he could ask a few personal questions before going into his lessons but he did not know how to ask the question. Deacon Taylor sensed the hesitation; "you seem to have something on your mind?" Lucious carefully organize his thoughts. "We don't have all day. Let it out," Deacon Taylor demanded. "First of all, this situation about the Gang Killers splashed across the news 24-7. It's bad enough, we are seen as killers but they are half my age. And you know Aaron, Trustee Jordan's son," Lucious asked as he whispered the information, thinking one of his guests would know who he was speaking of. Deacon Taylor made it clear by pointing to his ear and speaking loudly, "Boy, you are going to have to speak up if you want me to follow your story." Lucious tried repeating by yelling out the question but Deacon Taylor interrupted him, half way through, "I heard you. I'm not death, just speak a little louder. Now, what about Aaron? Yes, I do know him and his family," said Deacon Taylor. "He came to me a couple weeks ago about him and some Spanish kid in his school having a serious problem with one another." Lucious was being cautious as what he saying and not saying to Deacon Taylor, not sure if he was capable of handling certain issues a generation younger then himself were cooping with. Lucious had trouble with understanding the situation, so he knew Deacon Taylor would surely be out of the loop. Deacon Taylor blurred out, "him and that Spanish gang are about to kill each other and it is a matter of time." Lucious was shocked of his knowledge of the situation.

Deacon Taylor quickly gave Lucious a class on how it takes a village to raise a child. "You know, I live on the same block as him and the Spanish kid? Umh. Years ago, before you were born and before my legs gave out and I ended up in this wheelchair, I use to sit on my porch and watch the children play on my block. They would play so peacefully but when they would do something wrong or didn't play right, the parents would walk off their porch and go and correct those children. Parents then didn't question your authority but went and question that child but today... I no longer sit on my porch because if one of those kids start shooting at each other, I can't duck from a speeding bullet." Lucious had asked to be excused as he greeted a few guests but quickly came back and grabbed his seat.

Deacon Taylor without losing a beat continued speaking. "Today these parents will call you a liar in front of the child and the child will curse you out. I watch those boys do some ungodly things on my block. I watched a few of them kill one another. I might not sit on my porch but I do see some things from my bedroom window. Now, I'm not saying Aaron cursed me out because he shows me some respect and I'm not saying his mother called me a liar because she didn't, at least not to my face, she hasn't. But when that boy father had died a few years ago of cancer, I told his mother; her son was up to no good. And you know what she told me? She said to me, I got everything under control. That's what she calls, under control. You think you know your child but you really don't." Lucious could tell as Deacon Taylor spoke from experience.

"I spoke to Pastor Money about the situation; as well as my wife and they both have been tackling from two different angels. I have not spoken with Aaron since last week. I tried calling him but I get no answer and I didn't see him in church on Sunday." Lucious said to Deacon Taylor in concern. "Son, I spoke to Aaron, his mother, Pastor Money in a meeting and Trustee Jordan told me, 'I should have worried just as much about my own children; maybe they would have come out better.' You can only pray for that boy. If he doesn't want your help, you are wasting your time but I believe he is crying out for help. Maybe he will listen to you because he sure isn't listening to his mother or no old man in a wheelchair and he is going to end up killed if he keeps it up."

Friday night had rolled around. The temperature was warmer then usual on this fall dark evening. There were very few people wondering the streets of the neighborhood. Luscious was anxiously about to began the Rap Session as the young teenagers trickled into the church classroom. Deacon Taylor had been helping him immensely. Lucious' confidence was building and he seemed ready to walk into the young people's Rap Session and conduct a class for two hours.

Deacon Taylor and Lucious came up with the subject, topics and scriptures to back everything up so they were well thought out and executed. How the class was structured as well as what to look for from these young people is credited to Sarah. But Lucious could not help notice that a "saved" women's point of view was missing from the class. Meanwhile, Deacon Taylor requested Lucious to have his cooks at the restaurant prepare dinner for the kids.

Deacon Taylor chose to position his wheelchair off to the side, out of the way. He attempted to make young people comfortable in the setting but interjecting in the open discussion only when necessary. Lucious was appreciative of his mentors help. Deacon Taylor's presence in the class served three purposes to Lucious:

1. He had a strong knowledge of God's word.
2. Lucious and the younger members looked to him for guidance.
3. The older disgruntled members thought he would keep things in order.

So much has happen in the past two weeks that Lucious was not sure to be happy or disappointed with what seem to be ups and downs. One thing for sure, the young people rushed up to him after each Sunday service.

He counted about twelve young people, who have shown interest. The first class was an invitation to all the young people, a "NO PARENTS INVITED" sign was placed on the door. Deacon Taylor was confronted by one of the parents. Why can't we sit in and listen? He gracefully, assured them that children needed a safe place to let out steam without having to worry about their parents recording what they are saying. "I have your child's best interests at heart." Although the mother wasn't completely satisfied with his answer she reluctantly accepted it and moved on. Lucious chuckled as he recalled Trustee Jordan saying the same thing to Aaron and his boys.

Kids from all over began hearing about these Rap Sessions. Even college students expressed their interests; it was hard not including them in the class setting.

Lucious was not expecting much of an input from the church. Until Pastor Money included the following message on the announcement bulletin board: "The Rapture...We are preparing our children for the coming of the Lord. The young people will recognize it as a Rap Session, a place to rap about the real issues they are facing today. I like to think of it as a 'rights of passage', young people preparing themselves for adulthood." But when members laid eyes on the topic, everyone had an opinion. Lucious could not walk out of the church without having his coat tail pulled. The unenthusiastic older Christians out weighed the optimistic and animated younger Christians.

Pastor Money preached on the topic, which was posted in the church bulletin to help spark some energy and dialogue:

Yesterday's, March on Washington Voters vs. Today's, Driving to the Local Mall Voters. "Today's sermon comes from Esther; please turn with me to Esther 10:3 'Mordecai, who was Esther's uncle, was honored because he worked for the good of his people and stood up for their welfare…'. Shouldn't we also work for the good of our nation? I find these young people to be hopeless and confused." After the sermon an older woman with a mink coat and Gucci bag spoke as she greeted her sisters in the foyer of the church, "I do not understand why these young people can not get their acts together," She looked around the circle searching for an Amen. Simultaneously a man in the church choir leaned over to Lucious as if he was beckoning a response. "When we were children we listened and didn't think twice or else."

Lucious stood patiently waiting for Sarah to finish talking after service. He felt like he was being bombarded with negativity. And just when he needed it the most Deacon Taylor rolled up and gave him a few words of encouragement.

Deacon Taylor was one of the few older members who did not have anger in his voice. He had not been jaded. He was filled with the spirit of God. "These children aren't lazy they are too busy waiting to be lead by God knows who. When I was coming up racism was obvious and blatant and I thought I was escaping it when I moved up from the south. Children today deal with exponentially more than we did. They are confronted with racism, STD's, health issues, gangs, profiling and more. They are building more jails than school houses and capitalizing off of our kids' free labor. At least I knew who the enemy was; the hatred was in your face, but our poor kids don't know that the media and internet can be just as much their enemy and can be just as deadly. Lucious quickly placed a question on the table, causing Deacon Taylor to lose his train of thought. "What can we do to get our young people to understand all of this?" Deacon Taylor stopped for a second to get his thoughts together and like the expert he was, smoothly continuing on the subject.

"They must understand that they are Kings and Queens and the word must be clear. They want to know the truth and the ***Truth of the Matter*** is: everyone has been blowing smoke. We have to stop and get them to realize their purpose in life. Once our young people realize their potential, it will lead them to their purpose." Deacon Taylor had noticed the level of intensity in his own voice, which had jumped up a few notches. Lucious looked more alarmed by

Deacon Taylor's passion on the subject rather than the words that were coming from his mouth.

"Son, you, young people can be an unstoppable force. But what 'we' are doing is murdering our children because we are sending you all into the world unprepared for the danger that is much greater today than it was years ago. It's like Bush sending our soldiers into battle without truthfully telling them what they are up against and lying to them about what they are really there for. They're walking into a death trap and by the time they figure it out; the enemy already has them boxed in. We must strategize, if we are going to stop murdering our children's potential to be great. They must be prepared to fight the enemy and not be slaughtered.

Yesterday, when you walked out of your parents' door, you knew what to do, where to go, who to see, how to conduct yourself and what the outcome would be if you did not follow the simple rules. We had imposed limitations. Today, we are telling these kids that there are no limits, you can do anything, no one can stop you and the sky is the limit."

Deacon Taylor chuckled as he watched Lucious look at him for clarity; knowing Lucious was taught to think in such a way as a young Black man. "God says in

Philippians 4:13 I can do all things through Christ who straightens me.

We must teach our young people, in time, with faith and loyalty to Christ, they will as righteous men, inherit all the earth. Our young people need to guarantee their throne otherwise their kingdoms are doomed at such an unripe age. Before they become adults, the enemy is out to dethrone our children from which, what they are rightfully entitled." Deacon Taylor stopped to catch his breath but to make sure Lucious was following along. "So, there are no limitations through Christ." He said to Lucious in conclusion.

Deacon Taylor went on further to say, "Dr. Martin Luther King had a dream. He wanted our children to follow their dreams but the game has a new set of rules, and the rules change according to who is in charge of the way the game should be played. In some cases this may be true but at the end of the day we are saying, you are untouchable. You know what happens when you are untouchable in the world? Ask a celebrity, any famous person, anyone who is extremely wealthy, any nationally recognized person, and they will say they are all moving targets but they at least know how to protect themselves from the danger that is constantly surrounding them. Our children do not see danger. They are walking into pitfalls. They are not being protected and for them it is so simple. They do not need bodyguards, they do not have to carry weapons and they do not have to live in fear like some of these people they idolize tend to do."

Lucious was trapped in this old man's mouth waiting for the solution. He eagerly braced himself for Deacon Taylor's next words. He was not surprised about Deacon Taylor's simple answer. "The answer is the **Word**". He gazed at Lucious looking deep into his eyes. Deacon Taylor marveled; his apprentice was finally catching on. "If we are going to stop murdering our children they must know like we knew that the answers to all their questions lie within the Bible. Show them that there are limitations to everything in life. There are rules and consequences to everything in life. They are going to pay for everything one way or another. Freedom costs. It costs to be a Christian and the cost is greater not to be.

Men have taken people's lives because they believe in our Lord and Savior, Jesus Christ. But make no mistake, you'll pay and when you die it will be your soul that will be the commodity. God's natural resources are diamonds, oil, pearls and gold. They are the most expensive treasures on this earth. But He is trying to tell our young people not to fool themselves. Jesus has already paid the greatest price for Man."

Sarah walked over to her husband as if she was trying to save him from Deacon Taylor, who she knew to be long-winded, but Lucious was captivated by what he was saying. Sarah greeted both of them with a kiss on the cheek, "hello Deacon Taylor." Sarah's attempt to save Lucious from Deacon Taylor failed because Sarah got in on the conversation. As the both of them went back and forth in a great debate over today's youth, Lucious tried to focus but he was really thinking about something else. *Deacon Taylor is the oldest Deacon in the church, full of knowledge and understanding yet it's a shame more of my peers haven't sat down and talk to this man; and take advantage of his wisdom.*

Lucious always found it ironic that someone could grow up in a church and not really know people they had fellowshipped with for years. They could have crossed paths and not known they attended the same church or even served the same God for that matter. Deacon Taylor began to smile as he looked over at Sarah, while directing his words to Lucious, "I taught your wife you know. And some of my classes were heavy." Sarah smiled as she continued to rub her stomach. Lucious, meanwhile snapped out of what he was thinking and without having others realize he was not paying attention, he quickly responded to Deacon Taylor, "really."

Sarah had a great appreciation for her old high school teacher. She was fortunate to attend a school that focused on Christian education. "Dr. Taylor taught theology at my school." She continued, "He made you think and wanted us to debate because he knew in the end he would win by simply proving his case in the Bible." Deacon Taylor and Sarah laughed. Before they knew it, they were the only ones left in the church.

Part Seven

The second class is now in session at U2CGS (U-2 Can Get Saved Non Denominational Church). Deacon Taylor greeted everyone as his assistant rolled him in. He was swiftly moved to the back of the room where he could observe everything. Sarah joined the class only to be supportive to her husband. Like Deacon Taylor, Sarah had no intentions in participating in the class; but she and Lucious knew it was going to be hard for her to not say something for two hours in a day. Lucious politely pulled out a chair for his pregnant wife as Sarah took great honor in sitting beside Deacon Taylor. The kids piled in without incident.

Deacon Taylor immediately took notice. He wondered why every young person preferred to sit in the back of the class. He was taught to take off his hat before entering a building and young ladies were soft spoken and seen not heard. One young girl talked so much and so loud, Deacon Taylor wondered if she was talking to the boys next to them or the entire class.

Some of the parents walked their teenagers to class. They wanted to push the limits, but the rule was clear…no parents! The concerned parents wanted to be nosey. Lucious' restaurant staff quietly placed the food on a table in the back of the room. Trustee Jordan strolled in with beverages, hoping to be recognized and publicly thanked. "Aaron, please put these drinks on the table while I speak to Brother Bell, outside." Trustee Jordan was known for being a strong woman; she seemed to be in total control. She sat as a Trustee on several Boards and was extremely involved in the community. Despite her image, she stood in front of Lucious with fear in her eyes.

Lucious stepped outside the classroom to talk to Trustee Jordan. She handed him a check for one hundred dollars for the food on behalf of the church. "Brother Bell, first congratulations on the good news." She was speaking about his wife having a baby. "I appreciate how you have taken care of my son. Since my husband passed away, Aaron has been busy trying to find himself. As you can tell, I'm not the youngest mother and if that is not bad enough, I am a woman trying to raise a boy into a man." Lucious continue to listen as he looked at Aaron silently, reclining in his chair through the window of the door. "As of today, I've placed my son in a private school to get him away from the gangs.

I lost my husband. I refuse to lose my son to something stupid." She grabbed Lucious by the hand. "Only God decides when my son should leave me. Aaron is all I have on God's great planet. I'm sorry for the position you were placed in but you will see when your wife has your child. You will want to know everything so you can protect your child from any harm."

She hugged Lucious tightly and within a minute pulled it together and returned to her normal self, "Now, good luck. Go and teach our young people who God really is." All Lucious could say to himself was, *thank you God for whatever I've done because we need her support and prayer.*

Lucious walked into the classroom to find out, the class was already in a prayer circle waiting on him. "Yo! We are starving!" Isaiah, one of their young people in the class blurted out. "Great! Isaiah, can you please open us up in prayer and bless the food?" In his spontaneous shyness he said, "Come on Mr. Bell." Lucious laughed to himself while asking Deacon Taylor to bless the food.

After everyone was stuffed, Lucious doubted if he would have the young people's attention. It was clear they all knew one another from school or church; but he was unsure of three of their names. He had asked the class to go around the room and state their names, grade and to tell the class a little about themselves and what school they attended. Lucious formally introduced The Deacon and himself to the new faces.

Lucious continued to address the class. "You will need two things when you come to this class, your bible and respect." He opened the floor up to the students to find out what they expected from the class. Then he began, "Can someone tell me what affirmative action is?" The class looked around, no on knew the answer. "What does N.A.A.C.P. stand for? Who do you consider to be a Black National Leader? Have you ever been profiled? Is O.J. Simpson innocent? How do you really feel about being Black? Do you know who Jesus is? Do you have a relationship with God?" Lucious asked a series of rhetorical questions and had asked the young people to keep it real and to be truthful in their answers. "I am not here to preach and I do not know everything about the Bible. I have answers to each question I've asked you and I have a relationship with God. I'm as real as real gets about mine." Lucious simply let all the young people know that he was not there to impress them but to help them understand, he too was under instruction. Simply put, they were in the same boat.

"The subject is: March on Washington Voters vs. Local Mall Voters. Some of you are not old enough to vote but it is a very serious matter. This past election was conceded because a few people decided to stay home and not vote. They are the same people who are complaining about life. However, look at it as an opportunity -- an opportunity hundreds of millions of people in our world wish they had. It is called Democracy. Above all, pray for our nation during this crucial time. The Bible reminds us

Psalm 33:12 "Blessed is the nation whose God is the Lord."

"Is this generation going to vote in larger numbers, better yet, are you going to count? Everyone expects you, young people to understand your rights to vote but when it comes down to it, are you being taught how to vote? There are young men and women, who have served time in jail, who are unaware that they too are able to vote. Whose fault is this?" Aaron did not hesitate to throw his sense of humor, "it's their fault." The class began to laugh aloud. The class started to get a little rambunctious but Lucious managed to pull them back in.

"My mother said it doesn't make a difference." A voice yelled out over the class. It was Shemaiah, she embraced her individuality. Shemaiah was determined to be both seen and heard. Shemaiah's handmade version of Baby Phat clothes showed her love for fashion and being noticed. Lucious admired her courageous persona but knew he would have to deal with her scantly clad couture. Shemaiah's nails were painted royal blue. The tips of her hair were blue and her sneakers were blue. She had on a pair of jeans that were designed by Baby Phat and from the looks of it; they were eaten by the lawnmower. So, the question that Lucious kept asking himself, *is this trendy and hip? Because if this is considered the trendy way to dress, than there is no hope for the future.*

Lucious answered Shemaiah's mother's statement. "Your vote does make a difference." Lucious looked around the classroom addressing each person but personally directing his answer to Shemaiah. "We confuse the popular vote, which you and I cast our one vote between the Electoral College votes, in which each state cast their vote to elect the President of the United States. In the race for president, the winner of the electoral votes wins the oval office and the next President of the United States." The class jumped into an uproar.

Deacon Taylor and Sarah were surprised by the reaction of the class but were now paying very close attention to what was going on. "So, let me get this correct." Isaiah quickly said as he stood up, with his one finger pointing in the air. "Each one of the fifty states cast one vote and the candidates with the majority votes win the seat." Shemaiah tried to hold back her laughter because it was obvious Isaiah was trying to impress the class with his little knowledge in American History.

Sarah jumped into the conversation only to help explain. She knew when her husband was uncertain of things and as his wife she was there to fill in the blanks and to make sure her man always looked good. "Isaiah you are correct." Shemaiah quickly blurred out in the class "no he isn't correct because there are 51states not just 50. He's forgetting about the District of Columbia that is now a state." Sarah, Deacon Taylor and Lucious looked at Shemaiah because the topic and/or somebody was getting personal. Sarah attempted to continue to say something. "Shemaiah is correct and we thank her for that informative insight. "So, someone would have to win 26 votes." Isaiah shouted into the air. That's why I plan to run president in 2028 because that gives me enough time to get to know 51 people rather then three hundred million people. That's easy. That's life. All I have to do is cut out the middle man voters and find out those people on the Electoral College Board." "He's stupid." Shemaiah said.

"I guess I'll be president before him. Because him and the rest of his boys' doesn't know nothin'. That's why they'll be a woman as President before a man because you're all dumb." Lucious jumped in to stop the verbal fight. As their school teacher, Sarah was use to this sort of behavior. Deacon Taylor was laughing to himself because the energy over a Woman and Black man as the next President of the United States was pure oxygen in his blood. Sarah devilishly but not obviously took the side of the only young woman in a class. Sarah knew because of Shemaiah's get up, people took her less serious and judge her intelligence by the blue hair, sometime changing to blonde and red. They were quick to judge her level of astuteness the same way they treated Janet Jackson and her wardrobe malfunctions. The public census was full of loop holes. Did she really know what she was wearing or was she seeking attention? But Sarah knew as her teacher that Shemaiah had a secret weapon. With a little guidance, the right attention and plenty of love, Shemaiah would be unstoppable.

Sarah tried not to take over her husband's class. She was a visitor and she was not at the school teacher. "Mr. Bell, Honey, maybe

Shemaiah would like to explain to us about the Electoral College vote." Lucious looked carefully at his wife for clarity because *last time I remembered, Shemaiah was the person who caused this interruption in the class by making a statement about why they should not vote.* But Lucious knew his wife was making a point through one of her students. "Shemaiah can you please stand up and explain to us a little about the Electoral College vote." Sarah had asked and without any hesitation, Shemaiah stood just for the pure purpose to show the outfit she had made. Unlike Isaiah, Shemaiah was not concern about expressing her intelligence to anyone. Meanwhile, Sarah has been trying to explain to her students why they should go about proving how intelligent they were rather then try to impress one another on who was the most stupid.

"There are 538 total electoral votes. In order to win presidency he or she has to win 270 of those electoral votes. The electoral process was modified in 1804 with the ratification of the 12th Amendment. The Electoral College is administered at the national level by the National Archives and Records Administration and its Office of the Federal Register. The Presidential Electors meet in their respective state capitals in December, 41 days following the election, at which time they cast their electoral votes. Thus the "electoral college" never meets as one national body. They ballot for President, then ballot for vice president. Afterward, the Electors sign a document called the Certificate of Vote which sets forth the number of votes cast for these two offices and is signed by all Electors. Candidates must receive a majority of the electoral vote to be declared the president-elect or vice-president-elect." "Yeah, so how did they come up with 500 and something?" Isaiah questioned Shemaiah. Shemaiah said, "the amount of votes each state has depends on the population of each state." Sarah sat in her chair as she watched Shemaiah, *in her most outlandish outfit, the only young lady represented for the women in America as her follow young men try to keep up.* Lucious insincerely smiled over at his wife as he looked carefully at the young men to see if they were really following Shemaiah or not paying attention at all. *They probably could care less with what she's saying because her outfit alone takes all the attention and that's all young men at their age need; the wrong things to catch their attention.*

"So, the bigger the state or population the more votes that state carries. New York is a Blue state and we have 31 to Texas which is a Red state and they have 55 votes." Shemaiah said as the questions were flying from around the entire the class including Lucious and Sarah. "What is a Blue or Red State" asked Aaron. "A state that is

Blue is majority Democrat and a state that is Red is majority Republican. As you can see, Texas has more Electoral College votes then New York. So, if it was New York against Texas we would lose but there are 51 other states but the majority of them, I think are Red states, especially in the center of America." "So, Hillary Clinton and Barack Obama have no chance at all." Isaiah said. "That is not necessarily true, they just have it harder. Whoever can get the Red states to see past them being a Woman or a Black man and just see the person can possibly win the Presidency." Shemaiah responded as she impolitely smacked on her chewing gum. Isaiah turned to Shemaiah and asked, "What's up with all the blue are you representing the Democrats?" Lucious *wondered whether the entire class thought the same way or were they accustomed to Shemaiah and her fashion statements.* Her peers saw it as her way of expressing herself.

In a condescending voice, Shemaiah responded to Isaiah' question, "this is what you call Jay-Z Blue. See, you don't know anything about that." Now Lucious was really confused. Thanks to the rest of the class, he was given a one on one about the rich rap star's investments. Aaron attempt to educate Lucious on things about the world of a teenager, "Yeah Brother Bell, Jay-Z bought and patented especially made blue that is his trademark. Every company is using his color to market their products, even Crayola Crayons. Now, that's what you call buying power." Lucious was not impressed and could care less; no one was going to make him walk out the house looking like a clown. Lucious ran off the subject, to touch an area that the young people were feeling strongly about but reminded himself not to stray away from the topic too long as Deacon Taylor explained to him before. "I can not see Jay-Z wearing his own Jay-Z Blue suit to a business meeting at his age. Lucious said to the entire room. He continued to say things he'd hoped would get through to the young people but it was as if they were clueless. Again, whatever a character out of a movie or artist from the music industry says is like gold. Deacon Taylor without giving his opinion to the matter was curious. *Our children are not shown, there is a time and a place to wear a clown (blue) suit; and church was not the place but the Circus would be perfect.*

1 Peter 3:2-4, "He will see how you honor God and live a pure life. Do not depend on things like fancy hairdos or gold jewelry or expensive clothes to make you look beautiful. Be beautiful in your heart by being gentle

and quiet. This kind of beauty will last, and God considers it very special."

Before the class went down the path of no return, Lucious quickly jumped back into the subject. "Okay, Enough about Jay-Z because he votes. What do you think about the fact that our forefathers fought so hard to vote; yet less and less people today are voting? They have to pass a bill for you to continue to have the right to vote. What happens if the bill is not approved and your right is taken from you? Do have a choice of who is in office?" Lucious said hoping to spark some real emotions from the class, again. He got just that.

"I still feel they're going to put in office, who they want, so why stress yourself about it?" Shemaiah said. Isaiah abruptly interrupts, "people died for us to vote and too many people have paid the price for us. When I get old like Brother Bell and his wife, I plan not only vote but also one day, I will run for office. But why can't people vote on-line?" "EXCUSE ME, I'M NOT OLD." Sarah corrected Isaiah. Deacon Taylor interjected to break the ice and to save Isaiah from his impetuous statement. "Well, I'm old and I'm glad of it."

One minute Isaiah was very confident and in the next breath he questioned the possibility. "I don't think we will ever see a Black President, right Mr. B?" Lucious questioned how many others felt the same way as Isaiah. "Who agrees with what Isaiah just said?" Slowly the entire class raised their hands. They could not visually see a "Black" President in office. It was surprising to Lucious but to their senior visitor (Dr. Taylor) listening in, it was heart wrenching.

"I'll vote if Jay-Z runs for President of the United States," said one young person. "I will listen to Russell Simmons," said another. "Yo! No one makes more sense then fifty-Cent (Rap Artist)," said another. "I bet there'll be a woman in office before a Black President?" Shemaiah said out loud. As their voices went higher and debating who had more street creditability continued along with, who makes more money, who has more power and who has more respect. Deacon was quietly looking and pondering. *"Who were these people they so passionately speak of?"*

It was clear today's generation follow celebrities and believe more so in characters made up by the movies and music labels than they do in real leadership. "Why so?" Deacon Taylor and Lucious both asked. "Would the Deacon like to add to our discussion?"

Lucious quickly asked. Deacon Taylor, who normally is assisted by his male nurse, had heard enough. He expeditiously, with the help of his nurse, pushed his wheel-chair to the front of the room. His feeble body perked up with life; his voice spoke with the passion of a father, who was ready to scold a child for wrong doings.

"Have you not any mind what people have gone through for you? Have you heard of Senator Barak Obama? He could be the next Black President of the United States. Jesse Jackson ran for President. Al Sharpton took a stab at it." The entire class strangely looked over at the Deacon. "Okay he didn't have a chance. But who was the first Black President of the United States?" Again, the class strangely looked at the Deacon. "Former President Bill Clinton." The class burst into laughter.

It was as if the class was in the eye of a storm. The laughter and fun soon turned to a more serious matter. The storm abruptly changed its course and what came next could not be foreseen. Deacon Taylor eyes filled with water and with one blink of an eye the tears would flow down his wrinkled face. His lips began to quiver as he continued to speak as though he were talking to his own flesh and blood.

"I could have never imagined when I was your age any such thing. Now, all I can think of is how close the possibility of a Black President. It may even come before I leave this earth but it is possible. I refuse to see it any differently because what I now see is endless possibilities; and it is not because you cannot see it, you won't even try to see it! If that's the case, then you have no faith. You have to stop and think. If you cannot see what may seem impossible, then how will you be able to see who God is? You children can't even see what is in front of you. How can you see, who's around you?"

The tears he held back no longer hid themselves. He kept talking until the young people felt his heart. It was as if he had wanted to let it off his chest for sometime and never had a chance. He spoke for every person who fought for liberty. His body began to shiver and shake. Lucious politely signaled the elderly assistant to push him from the front. The assistant was not much younger than Deacon Taylor. Deacon Taylor's assistant was a man of few words and a great listener. Lucious as well as the class almost forget he was there. "Do. Not. Move. Me." Deacon Taylor demanded. Deacon Taylor was far from finished.

"You all have to learn how to avoid using your natural senses to understand some things about God. You have to connect yourself with your spiritual senses. Your survival depends on it; your salvation depends on it." He was right when he said he was not finished because he had a testimony or more like a sermon prepared for this day.

"He who spares the rod hates his son, but he who loves him is careful to discipline him," he quotes the Bible perched up in the front of the room. "I love you children and God knows you are all dealing with some things I have not had to deal with, because I do not understand your world. I may not relate but I'm here to help discipline you in your walk with Christ.

I will tell you all a secret. I was once a young man. But I do not want anyone of you to go through what I had to go through to appreciate who God is. But regardless of my struggle, I know God lead me out of it all as he has done with Moses and his people.

The Bible says, God spoke to Moses and said, **go in to Pharaoh, and tell him,** "This is what God says, **'Let my people go, that they may serve me.'** See, years ago my family was a sharecropper. Sharecroppers, in a sense, leased the farmland. They grew crops on another person's land and paid a fee, like a lease agreement but kept whatever they grew. The disparity was in the excessive costs of leasing the land and the unfair purchase prices of their crops. However, in some cases, the lease terms were so unfair that it was one step from slavery. Sharecroppers worked on a plantation and were paid very little. Yes, it was a form of slavery. You thought you owned a small piece of the land but the system was set up for you to always be in debt. Similar to credit cards of today."

Aaron had raised his hand to ask a question but like the rest of the class, he was afraid to interrupt Deacon Taylor and his great story. "Yes, my son." Deacon Taylor said. "So, you lived in the projects?" Aaron asked with all seriousness. "EXACTLY." Deacon Taylor tried to shout out from his weak body. "It was hard to get out of sharecropping just as hard as it is for a family to get out of low income housing, projects. But worst. They were willing to kill you to keep you there. If you'd left, who would take care of the fields? They didn't make any money and if they didn't make any money then how would they be able to eat.

One day my father had gone in town to vote but the power at hand was there to intimidate him. He was not mentally afraid but still, he was physically hurt and wounded while he tried to vote. When he was bought home, all my Mama could thank God for was her husband was not lynched or mistaken as a piece of blood fruit hanging from a tree as Billy Holiday had said in her song. She was mentally afraid for my father's life and much as she tried to keep him from acting as Nat Turner had done during slavery. Figuratively speaking, I thought my father was greater then life because he was not afraid of anything or anyone. Isaiah's finger went up in the air, "who is Nat Turner?" "Young man, you've asked a great question. Nat Turner was an American slave whose failed slave rebellion in Virginia, was the most remarkable instance of black resistance to enslavement in the antebellum southern United States. His methodical slaughter of white civilians during the uprising makes his legacy controversial, but he is still considered by many to be a heroic figure of black resistance to oppression. Though he became known as "Nat Turner" in the aftermath of the uprising, his actual given name was simply "Nat".

"Thank you." Isaiah said. "But as I was saying about my father, Mr. Smith, the owner of the land came to our house and told my mother, on my father's death bed that we still owed him and with or without my father we still had to work the field. My father died that night. They killed my father but they did not kill his dream.

My mother did not cry in front of any of her seven children, she simply told the man, 'yes' and returned to my father's bedside. I was only sixteen then and God came to me that night. I was the youngest of five boys but I had two sisters that were younger than me. But like Moses told Pharaoh to let his people go, I told my mother what was said to me. God told me, 'we were going to leave the south and I was supposed to help my mother move.' She in return went to Mr. Smith and told him that my Daddy did not owe him anything and he must let us go debt free. Mr. Smith scoffed at my mother's request.

My mother had a choice to make; she could stay and continue to live in debt with no hope of ever having it lifted, or we could run in search of a better life and pray Mr. Smith couldn't track us down. I buried my Daddy the next day. The next week my mother, two younger sisters and I made a journey to New York. She left my four older brothers in the south. I never asked my mother but she left my brother behind for a few reasons, they were men, she couldn't tote all of us and Mr. Smith wasn't trying to hear letting everyone go because then he would have to work the fields in that hot sun. "

At the end of his story there was silence. Not a word was said until the class clown spoke, "may we have a moment of silence," said Aaron. Shemaiah asked, "Was your mother afraid?" Isaiah asked, "Did you already have family in New York?" A strange smile came across Deacon Taylor's face.

"After my father's death, my mother was a new woman. She was not afraid. I thought for years she had put on a good face to keep her children from worrying. But before my mother left this earth, she told the story of how she feared no man because she had faith. No, we did not have any family but we moved in with one of my mother's good friends. She had two children and had left the south a few years before. We stayed there for about seven months. Can you imagine how tight that apartment was? Well, we didn't complain, because the house we grew up in was even worse. And back then you could not call Child Protective Services or 911 on your parents." The class laughed.

Sarah gave the class a chance to run and for Deacon Taylor to end on a great note. "Excuse me Deacon Taylor, if I may. Is there anyone who would like to use the lady's or men's room before Deacon Taylor concludes and Lucious gives us a closing prayer?" Lucious was not good as his wife at picking up clues, "this is an intermission." He said with a smile as if he said something differently than Sarah. "Brother Bell, I think everyone is okay, if you'd let Deacon, here finish, we'll be ready to escort ourselves to the little lady's room." Shemaiah said with a smirked with an evident sign of impoliteness as she looked over at Sarah for rudely interrupting Deacon Taylor's story. *Oh! No she didn't*, Sarah thought to herself as she kindly gave Shemaiah a returned ill-mannered grin with no teeth appearing.

"Excuse me Deacon Taylor did you share a room with your siblings and your mother?" Shemaiah asked in a sign of discuss. Deacon Taylor in a kind way avoided the question. His audience would not understand the sacrifice his mother had made. "No one had their own room and if you did not like it then you'd run away and no one would go looking for you, you just reappeared after you realized it was harder out there, than in a crowded two bedroom apartment. I know because I tried it. Well...my mother found a job as a housekeeper. She remarried and shortly after we moved to Long Island."

Like the teenagers who paid close attention, Lucious was curious, yet blown away. "Deacon Taylor was that the hardest thing you had to deal with in life?" The big smile went across his face, again. He took a second to respond, which indicated he endured much. "No, I have dealt with much harder things in life. Just because you are saved doesn't mean life will always be easy." His young audience was confused. "You are better at handling the problem, but before being saved the problems seem to always handle you." Sarah knew as a student of Deacon Taylor's that any subject is liable to turn into a lengthy dialogue. She shot Lucious with a piercing look to insist he stop Deacon Taylor from starting another topic or story.

Lucious helped Deacon Taylor bring the class back to it original topic. "Deacon Taylor we were discussing the subject: Marching Voters vs. Local Mall Voters. Do you have anything you would like to add to this?" Lucious asked Deacon Taylor. His wife and Isaiah shot a look at him for setting them and everyone else up for another hour of PBS series. "I marched on Washington because I wanted something great out of life." Deacon Taylor began to say. "I'd faced my hardship and demons and that is what makes me smile.

When my father was killed for voting, he paid the price for me to vote. I didn't understand Christ death and the price he paid for all of us but when your biological father pays for your freedom with his life then everything else seem bearable. ***The Truth of the Matter is***: You will go through some things but right now it seems tough. It may seem unbearable but the day you accept Christ, some things that are so hard will still be hard but you will be able to persevere. You'll be able to go away with battle scars that only you will see as beauty marks because you will know how you battled your demon and won. Unsaved people will see you struggle and wonder why you smile. Just like some of you wonder as I tell my story. You wonder how I could smile. Every time I go to vote, I think about my father."

Deacon Taylor called on Shemaiah to direct every word he was saying toward her heart and mind. "Look, it may not seem important to you to vote, but it is shameful to make our fight in vain. We fought hard for a right we were denied because of the color of our skin and you all take this for granted. That is okay, but do not think all things last forever. Somebody has to stand on the front line and somebody will die for the lifestyle you live. So I ask you this; the life you have, is it worth dying for or is your life worth nothing? My father stood on the front line and died for me to vote. Someone is standing on the front line in Iraq for you to have the freedom to live in a free world. But don't forget one thing; Jesus gave his life for you. So, all these people paid a price with their lives for you'll to wonder if you should or shouldn't vote."

Lucious was able to take what Deacon Taylor had said and get the class to understand, "Our young people have no clue what some of our older Black organizations stand for or if they still even exist. You all can't tell me what N.A.A.C.P. stands for or means to you?" The class seemed insulted but no one was quick to give him an answer. "How many of you would march or picket down the street because of unjust issues happening in your community?" Isaiah again was ready to throw out his response. "I would march if I knew Beyoncé was marching beside me."

"National Association for the Advancement of Color People is what N.A.A.C.P stands for. This organization is fighting for young people like you; the only problem is the members that were there in the 50's and 60's are still there, today and not enough of our young people of today are joining the fight. Deacon, would you like to add anything to this class before we rap things up?" Deacon Taylor looked around at the class. Sarah, Aaron and Isaiah looked at one another as if to say, *if you give Deacon another word, we will never leave.* Deacon Taylor began to cough forcefully. He shook his head and declined. Aaron and Isaiah let out a long sigh and jumped from their seats. "I do have one question." Deacon Taylor strained his voice to speak. "What does it take to get through to all of you, in this class?" The class looked around at each another to see who was willing to answer the question. Shemaiah sounded off as a passionate, concerned young person but showing no sign of disrespect. Her point was well taken, as she seemed to let an issue off her mind. "We don't care about how much y'all know until we know how much y'all care and as far as I'm concern no one's checkin' for us. Y'all want us to act one way but how do you know how to act if no one's teaching you how to act. These people in this church can say what they want but I handle mine. No one's handlin' nothin' for me. So when y'all busy saying we are not on the front line fighting the same battle, I want one of y'all to walk in my shoes around my way. I have to fight off these dumb, disrespectful, good for nothin', low life men on my block and then fight my mama, my teachers, you older people in the church and still have enough energy to get good grades, pass with flying colors and hopefully make somethin' of myself."

Sarah swiftly ran over to Shemaiah to escort her out of the room as Shemaiah broke out in tears. Sarah wrapped her arms around Shemaiah as Shemaiah attempted to shield her face and her tears with Sarah's body.

"If there are no other questions, I would like to tell you our next class is two weeks from today, same time. Please copy my e-mail and phone number down. Lucious prepared to dismiss the class and to remove the attention off Shemaiah's melt down.

Shemaiah pulled herself together and as if nothing had happen, she jumped back into the class. "Deacon Taylor, Brother and Sister

Bell, I'm sorry for that but I had that on my mine for a while." Shemaiah was able to laugh at outburst, "that was my rendition of Fantasia playing Celie's character in the Broadway play, Color Purple. But whatever happened to Mr. Smith, the land owner?" The class stopped as they all looked in the direction of the Deacon to hear his answer. Aaron and Isaiah looked at each other, then at Shemaiah and realized there could be no short answer for such a good question. They sat back down without a fight.

Deacon Taylor tried finishing the story despite his incessant coughing, "A year later Mr. Smiths' entire crop died from a dry season, the year after that there was a flood. He eventually died, leaving his wife and son to care for the land. His son moved away, leaving Mrs. Smith to try to do her best on her own." One of the young people, directed by Lucious, graciously passed Deacon Taylor a glass of water. Deacon Taylor continued, "My four older brothers and their families plowed her land. My family took good care of Mrs. Smith. Unfortunately, she later died, and when she died, she left my four brothers all her land. She left the land to my brothers but her son, Junior fought hard to remove my family off that land. And even when she willed her land to my brothers, believe you me, if that son of hers' had not died, they would have taken that land and given it back to him. But back then, they would force you off the land or see that you could not pay the taxes and then take it. But bless his heart, Mrs. Smith son died in his sleep. God don't like ugly.

Mrs. Smith was very helpful to Blacks. She was the only white person I came to know during those days who would risk her life to teach Blacks how to read and write. Mr. Smith forbade her, but she just kept on teaching. Now, part of the one hundred acres of land has the town high school in honor of Mrs. Smith. On the other eighty acres, one of my nephews built a big house for his family. Now my nephew in South Carolina is the Superintendent of that school district." The class was entranced by Deacon Taylor's story. "Can you believe we once walked away from that land? That is how God works.

John 8:24 "We must believe. Finally, there are those who have faith but they are letting their faith slip away."

The young people stood on their feet as they applauded Deacon Taylor and his story explaining why he continue to fight for the right to vote and how voting meant life or death to him. Without another word Deacon Taylor had his assistant roll him from the class. Lucious was left to give closing remarks and prayer.

"This generation is accustomed to fast food, fast cars, cutting edge technology, having material things, digital cameras, cell phones, computers, etc. and when this generation goes to vote, you are surprised the voting machines have not caught up to today's technology. Yesterday, they were denied the right to vote and today, you take your right to vote for granted because voting is an inconvenience. Well, if you do not stand up and put Jesus first, then imagine what the outcome will surely be."

Lucious was finished and drained by the end of the two-hour class. "Sarah could you close us on in prayer." Sarah was happy the class was over because she was more drained than Lucious. Her feet started to take a turn for the worst and just when she was finally was comfortable in her seat after dealing with Shemaiah's, she was ready to give a short prayer and continue walking toward her car without saying goodnight.

"Father, God, in the name of Jesus. We thank you for these young people. We are thankful for Deacon Taylor's wisdom and guidance. We're thankful for my husband dedication and willingness to help our young people. We say thank you for allowing us to be able to discuss in a positive manner, our differences; what and how we can achieve our purpose in life. We pray that each and every one of your young people are able to take something tonight with them that will cause them to think in a better way. I pray they will continue to come to this class to receive your word. I pray that they will be leaders and not followers. I pray for their deliverance. I pray that they understand why they should vote and not take voting for granted. I pray that they will understand through you, all things are possible. They will do things according to your will and way. We give you the glory and the honor. Amen." They prayed and the class was over.

Part Eight

A half an hour after the forum was dismissed Lucious, bumped into Aaron who is standing in the lobby of the church. He was patiently waiting for his mother to come out of a Trustee meeting in another part of the church. "Are you waiting on your mom?" Lucious asked.

"Yeah." Lucious found this the best time to talk, although Aaron had recently started working in the restaurant. "The last time you and I talked, the kid in the gang from down the street was locked up for bringing a weapon to school. Did you all settle your differences?" Away from his peers in the class, Aaron was lost for words. He was expressionless. His answers were short. "Yes". "No". Nodding and shaking his head. "No," he replied. Lucious said to him, in an attempt to understand Aaron's anger, "according to my wife, the problem with the gangs in your school has probably escalated, since those kid's went on a killing spree and acted like they were in a Scarface movie?" Aaron stood there cold and silent.

If Aaron did not know Lucious, he probably would have told him to go somewhere, but his body language was saying it for him. "It seemed as though you have nothing to say but when you are ready to talk, you'll let me know," Lucious said. Just then, Trustee Jordan walked up.

It was clear that she and Aaron had some unfinished business. The tone in her voice was much different from the one she had at the classroom door. "That meeting was long." She said as she placed her car keys in Aaron's hand. "Aaron, go to the car. I have something to discuss with Brother Bell." Aaron walked out of the church but not without first sarcastically thanking Lucious. "Thanks. The next time I need help, I know who not to call." Trustee Jordan, quickly intervened, apologizing for her son, "Excuse him."

She waited for Aaron to walk a good distance before saying anything, "he is not happy about me transferring him to a private school but besides his education, I have to worry about his safety. This hardly guarantees my child safety and my problem is still there. I think things have gotten worse. I do not want to bother you with my problems. I'm a mother trying my best, to keep my child from getting killed on the streets, over some non-sense. Now, I have to worry about gangs." Trustee Jordan caught herself as she realized, her frustration was being taken out on Lucious. "I can tell he's been trying to strengthen his spiritual side but his natural side seems to be getting out of control. One minute he's the perfect kid in the church, the next minute he's putting his life or someone else's in danger."

She thought about what she had just said and for a second she found a slight bit of humor in the **Truth of the Matter** is*: sounded like half the members in the church, you know church folks. Saints on Sunday but Hell raisers the rest of the week. She found herself chuckling.* "But I have to do more than just pray. Does this mean I have no faith?" She asked Lucious as if he was the person with the answer to her question.

"What am I suppose to do, Brother Bell?" She asked rhetorically. He could do nothing but listen. Unexpectedly, tears began streaming down her face. She was not expecting an answer. It seemed as though she was searching God for answers. "Trustee Jordan, is there anything I can do for you?" He asked, hoping for a small assignment from a woman known to haze a Brother.

"Thank you, Brother Bell. Yes, you can help me. I need you to give my son plenty of hours in your restaurant. I want to know everything about these gangs in our town. I want to know how deeply involved, my son is? I am going to call the Mayor; this can't be put off any longer. I want to know what is being done about all of this." Lucious was willing to help but he didn't want to get in over his head.

As Pastor Money headed to his brand new Jaguar parked in his personal spot; Trustee Jordan quickly dried her tears and replaced them with a masquerading smile. Whether he liked it or not, Lucious was on assignment. He would have to find out everything that Aaron knew. It was weighing on him like a ton of bricks. Trustee Jordan's sorrow seemed to be transferred to him. Pastor Money approached. "Brother Bell, are you okay?

Part Nine

Christmas was near and Sarah was just beginning to enjoy her pregnancy. Baby and Parent Magazines replaced Sarah's Essence and Elle Magazines throughout the house. Sarah began to modify the furniture while Lucious found himself baby proofing the entire house. What little spare time he had was either spent painting a baby room or walking through Baby's R US. It seemed like just yesterday they were picking out curtains for their new home. Now he was being subjected to choosing between different high chairs, cribs, strollers, baby furniture and playpens. To him they were all the same, but for Sarah, she was on cloud nine. He found time to crack a smile and have a second wind when his voluptuous wife pranced around the house.

As busy as the restaurant kept him, it seemed Lucious was beginning to take on more than he could handle. Aaron had been working more diligently than some of the adults at the restaurant. He was eager to learn and always aimed to please the guests. He had a goal to buy a car by the end of the school year, rather than drive his mother's newly purchased 500 series Mercedes around town. Lucious thought at first he would have to fire the kid in a week and explain to his mother why she should worry. But Aaron not only grew on Lucious but also had a spark about him. He was looking for something and working at the restaurant was more of his safe haven or hide out.

Here Lucious was sitting alone in the restaurant after a busy night had gone by, glaring out the frosted windows. The snow had fallen lightly on the ground. The streets were empty and the hour was late. Kelly Price's melodic voice coursed through his soul, singing his wedding song, "Proposed." His eyes teared up as he remembered Sarah walking down the aisle. His thoughts were going everywhere but he could not help but realize how blessed he really was.... With all that God had given him, what was he to do when his child was placed in his arms? A gift like no other, it would be his to cherish. He wanted God to bless him in all his areas of weakness; as a Christian, husband and now as a father. His biggest prayer was to receive patience. He held tightly on his pocket Bible and wept as he reached his hands to heaven hoping for God to answer. A couple of hours later, he was walking threw his front door with everything fresh on his mind.

Lucious noticed as he walked into his bedroom Sarah was curled up as a baby in their bed and fast asleep. Lucious stood in the door of their bedroom and for minutes and stared in at his wife, the curves of her body protruding from the blanket. He gently placed the quilt completely over her body before he could sneak away to undress himself, she softly greeted him.

"Hi, Baby." She said as if her eyes were closed but she was far from sleep. It was dark, but he could hear from her voice she was pleased her husband was home. Lucious felt a chill in the house, but she told him not to go anywhere. The thermostat could wait. He undressed and hurried in the bed and closely cuddled with her, trying to absorb her body heat. They tucked under the cover as though they were trapped in the wilderness with no heat and just each other to keep warm. As Lucious began to get comfortable he noticed she was asleep. With disappointment, he turned on the heat and climbed back into bed.

"Lucious?" She whispered. "What's up Sarah?" "Are you afraid of fatherhood?" He was silent for a minute before answering the question. "I want our child to have the best and I do not want our child to go without." The sound of fear crept through her voice. "You know my mom was my mother and father. I recall my mother working two jobs to give us a decent life and paying for private schools. If there is one prayer I always made to God, it was to allow my child to have a father figure. I don't know what it feels like to have a dad around, so I know I will cherish my child's moments with you. I love you." Lucious did not have anything to say but "I love you, too."

Sarah gave Lucious every opportunity to make love to her. Lucious did not always get the message but he understood Sarah's call. Only during intimacy did Sarah allow Lucious to man handle her. She enjoyed pretending to be taken advantage of. She wanted to be chased. She seized the moment and if he did not comply, then off with his head. He fulfilled her wish and they became one in the flesh. Normally, he feared the worst after having sex, getting his wife pregnant at the wrong time. So, when he would reach his climax he would break the bond. But she was already pregnant. The fear in having sex was removed. The blanket laid on the side of the bed as the temperature crept up. Sweat poured from their bodies, as his wife submitted too his manhood. They released in unity and embraced each other with out sacrifice. He gently placed the blanket over her naked body, which showed her silhouette. He held his wife and from his deep thoughts he drifted into a deep sleep.

Proverbs 5:18-19 *"Let your manhood be a blessing; rejoice in the wife of your youth. Let her charms and tender embrace satisfy you. Let her love alone fill you with delight."*

Part Ten

L ucious sat in his restaurant late in the afternoon reading a local Christian Based Newspaper, "Stand Up Ministry" of Long Island. The news article within the paper had captured his attention. "Shut Up and Lead," it was titled, written by a seventeen year old boy, who lived with his mother and had recently been saved.

Shut up and lead

My name is Emmanuel Jones and I'm seventeen. I go to Bishop Edgar A. Love H.S. I'm one of the top students in my senior class. I enjoy learning, church, God, reading the Bible, my friends, life and helping other people. I do not know my father, but my mother did the best she could. What she supply's me with is not enough, but I do not complain because I know one day what is owed to me I will surely receive. Nevertheless, I would like the local politicians in this area to know why I put my faith only in God and not people.

The entire nation is making money off us from the time we are born as Young Black people. My social worker gets a paycheck in order to try to keep us "babies from having babies." The schools get additional money for every dysfunctional, mental or socially challenged student. According to them I fall into one of those categories but I show no signs. The police department gets overtime on top of their paycheck to oversee my friends in the street, which are far from safe. The correctional facilities get to offer their most valued employees six figure salaries to keep me from killing my own, while the big time companies get free labor and still make a profit. You take my right to vote, my equal rights, right to work, my manhood, my family, my dignity and then expect me to become someone. The liquor store and drug dealers are set up to help us drink and smoke our lives away. The lobbyists, who do not have my best interest in mind, get big money to keep my vote from counting. The music and movies make my friends stupidly believe they can afford the same lifestyle as a Hip-Hop artist. With all the money being put out to make sure I never succeed in life, what makes anyone think I have a chance? That's why I have faith in God, only.

Lucious felt the pain of the kid and the article was so heartfelt. He decided to call the paper to reach the parent of the kid and to see if he could offer him a job. He contacted a good friend/owner of the publication, "Ted, this is Lucious. I just finished reading an article written by...." Before Lucious could finish his sentence, Ted was already saying the kids' name. "You're speaking about, Emmanuel Jones. He is a very talented kid and one day he will be in a pulpit, preaching to the next generation" Lucious thought the kid sounded like he did once. He remembered the day when he moved with passion and spoke from the heart about working with the youth. God spoke to Lucious at an early age, "I will use you to help teach others and spread the gospel." But Lucious went for years denying his conversation with God. Until the announcement of his wife and him having a child, he thought he had everything planned.

Lucious was starting to think while on the phone with Ted, about his purpose in life. "I want to give the kid a job, if he is interested in working" It was not the first time someone had prophesized to him and said the same thing. "I'm available all day. I will be here in the restaurant; have him come by or call me before I leave." Ted could not let Lucious off the phone before enticing him with a little more of Emmanuel's gift of writing. "I will e-mail you a piece he's written for us for next week. But if you've been reading the paper, you would have noticed his articles in the past editions. Where have you been, Brother?"

Lucious was saved by the bell; his cell phone was ringing. It was his wife. "Ted, I have to go, it's my wife and I did read last week's paper." Before Lucious could hang up the phone, Ted promptly rebutted, "Sure. Tell the Mrs. I said, hello." Lucious grabbed the phone but Sarah did not sound like herself. "Is everything okay?" He asked. "Lucious, Deacon Taylor is in the hospital. My mother said that he's in Winthrop Hospital." Lucious was silent for a minute. "What's wrong?" He asked in distress. "I'm not sure."

Part Eleven

A week before Christmas and Deacon Taylor has to spend his holiday in the hospital. Lucious drove to the hospital to see if he could visit his mentor. He left the restaurant in the hands of Aaron. Lucious trusted Aaron to run the restaurant in his absence because at times he was more mature and trustworthy than some of the adult employees. He only prayed he would have a business when he returned. "I'm here to visit Doctor Richard Taylor." The ninety year old volunteer gave a welcoming smile. "Are you family?" Lucious smiled back and quietly stuttered, "N-N-No."

"Sorry darling, immediate family only," she said in a dismissive way. Her polite smile shifted as her true personality was revealed. Lucious began to remind himself, not every elderly woman is a Christian. "He's my dad." The volunteer who could be the perfect President of the National Seniors dropped her head and glanced at Lucious with one raised eyebrow. Her disciplinary look gave Lucious an uncomfortable feeling. She saw passed his white lie. "Come Again?" The spunky elderly volunteer insisted. Lucious knew he was in trouble.

As Lucious turned to leave the nursing station he saw Pastor Money and another gentleman approaching. The debonair pastor briefly spoke to the volunteer. As she gladly handed him a piece of paper with Deacon Taylor's room number written on it. "Good to see you, Pastor." Pastor Money began to address Lucious. "Brother Lucious, this is Deacon Taylor's son." Lucious quickly sized him up. He wasn't what Lucious had expected. Lucious imagined that the mentor he had been spending so much time with in recent months would surely have reproduced great professors, engineers, ministers, doctors or businessmen to carry on his legacy. After shaking the gentleman's hand Lucious thought, *God forgive me for judging this man, he could be any of those things for all I know.*

Lucious proceeded down the hall with them but quickly stopped in his tracks and looked over at the feisty elderly volunteer. The volunteer glanced at Lucious, "And Oh! You may go but don't try that, again. Boy, I have grandchildren your age. I've seen and heard it all." Pastor Money and Dr. Taylor's son looked at each other then at Lucious. Lucious did not entertain them, instead speeded onto the elevator.

Truth Of The Matter

The men walked into the room to see Deacon Taylor, lying on the bed pleasantly talking with his doctor. Deacon Taylor's face lit up when he saw his visitors. He introduced the doctor to his guests. "Doc. This is my Pastor. Pastor Money." Deacon Taylor looked over at his son. "This is my son Abraham." He introduced his son with no life in his voice, no excitement, as if he was trying to keep a well hidden secret. "This young minister is Brother Bell; he is doing great things for the Lord. He doesn't know but he shall soon see." The smile on Deacon Taylor's face said a thousand words as a father who is proud of his son. His smile showed great pride. Maybe, Lucious had reminded him of himself.

Lucious shook the doctor's hand but corrected the Deacon. "I'm no minister." Deacon Taylor was a man who saw greatness and had a clear way of knowing and seeing God's work before anyone else. God had given him a vision about Lucious, which Deacon Taylor would not take lightly but as the truth. The Pastor smiled but Abraham interrupted the awkwardness.

Abraham interjected with a few words, "I heard about the work you've been doing in the church. Those young people need men like you. If dad gives you credit then accept it, because he's a tough old man," he said as he looked in his fathers face for a reaction. But there was none. "Your father is a great man. I've always known your dad but in the last few months, I really got to know him. Now, he's my mentor."

Lucious did not know what he said wrong, but Abraham suddenly walked out of the room. Pastor Money did not miss a beat and without acknowledging his dear friend son's disappearance, he was mindful of his busy schedule and quickly asked to pray. Lucious jogged into the waiting area to catch up with Abraham as the two old men talked church business. There Abraham was staring out of the window, deep in thought.

He walked over to where Abraham was standing. His clothes were old and tattered. His teeth had decade. His skin was abrasive. Deacon Taylor and his wife were both very focused on their careers; as a result they had Abraham very late in life. He was just few years older than Lucious, yet his hard life left him looking aged. At a glance, the scars on his face and the chip in his tooth seemed to tell his story. With further scrutiny Lucious saw the evidence of years of drug abuse; there were tracks on his arms and between his fingers. Although the wounds had healed long ago the scars remained to tell the story. "It's a blessing to see your Dad recovering" Luscious said. "Yeah! He's a fighter." They stood in momentary silence as they gazed out the window. "Lucious, is your name?" Abraham asked. "Yes." "Learn what you can from my father. He has a lot to teach, if you are willing to listen. He has God in his heart and he will never steer you wrong. Too bad I figured it out so late. Now, all I can try to do before he leaves this earth is to hope he will see some of the changes I've made in my life." Abraham went over to push the button for the elevator.

Lucious respected the fact that Abraham wanted to prove he had become a new man. He, however, was afraid if Deacon Taylor were to leave him. All the questions about the Bible, being a Christian and fatherhood would be left up to him to find out on his own. His father and mother had divorced when he was a child and he did not have a great relationship with his father. In Lucious' mind he could care less if his father was displeased by his action, so he wondered how it felt to want your father's acceptance.

Lucious did not think he was capable of teaching the class without Deacon Taylor's guidance. As the numbers lit above the elevator door, God came into the midst. Lucious was surprised at what came from his mouth to Abraham's ears. "Since you know your earthly father to be the man he is, wouldn't he be more proud to see whether or not God your heavenly father notices the change in your life?" The elevator door closed separating the two men as they parted without saying another world. Lucious prayed the strange man, the son of a great man and the once lost soul, would also receive the message he had himself received.

Part Twelve

The restaurant was still standing and everything seemed under control as Lucious walked through the doors. The guests were happy. Lucious called out, "Okay, Aaron get ready to leave; and I want to see you this evening at Rap Session." "I'll be there Lou. So how's the Deacon? Can I go with you next time, to visit him?" Aaron asked. "No problem. I'm pretty sure he will like that, but let's wait until he comes home. Let him get well and we'll take a ride to his house together. Okay? He probably won't be at Rap Session for a while." Aaron began to frown. "Oh a'ight," Said Aaron. At that moment Lucious realized Deacon Taylor had impacted more lives than just his.

The wisdom Deacon Taylor acquired throughout his life could only be achieved by living those life experiences or they could be transferred from someone insightful, to someone like Lucious, who was eager to draw from the wealth of knowledge that Deacon Taylor possessed. Lucious had come to learn more about the bible, about history and about himself. It was Deacon Taylor's grandfatherly presence that influenced the lives of everyone he encountered. Both Aaron and Lucious wondered how his absence would affect the Rap Sessions.

Lucious began to survey the restaurant when he noticed a young man waiting in the foyer. "A representative from the department of health is waiting for you?" Aaron asked as he looked over at the young man in a business suit. "Good evening Mr. Bell. I am Emanuel Jones. I hope this isn't an inconvenience." As the young man extended his hand, Lucious silently admired his presentation. He wore a suit and held a small black binder containing his résumé and a pen. The boy was well spoken and clean cut. "Uhmm, yes, good evening Emanuel. It is an honor to meet you as well." "Yes Mr. Bell, it is. I was asked by Mr. Ted Peters of 'Stand Up Ministries' newspaper to come by and speak with you." It was refreshing for Lucious to see there were some young people who understood the true meaning of preparation.

Lucious stared closely at Aaron then at Emmanuel. As Aaron turned and walked away he sucked his teeth and murmured "preacher's kid," before disappearing into the back. "Aaron, you know Emmanuel from your old school, right?" Aaron looked Emmanuel over. "Nah, I don't remember him." Lucious didn't play into Aaron's childishness.

"No? Okay well then can you get me and ... Mr. Jones something to drink?" Aaron glared at Emanuel and sarcastically answered "Yes Sir. No problem, Sir."

James, the evening manager entered the restaurant. Lucious and Emanuel had been speaking for a little while when, James' arrival clued Lucious in on the time and left him wondering how he would make it through that nights' Rap Session without Deacon Taylor. Although he and Deacon Taylor had gone over some topics a few days earlier, Lucious did not feel confident about leading the class on his own. He knew that the teenagers would test his abilities. As he continued to contemplate the future of the Rap Session, Emanuel interjected. "Is everything okay, Mr. Bell?" He found himself explaining the situation to Emanuel, eager to hear the young man's point of view.

Aaron finally returned with two glasses and a pitcher of ice water. Instead of just dropping it at the table, he took the opportunity to chime in. "Yo! Lucious! I was on the computer last night searching for scriptures that relate to everyday life. I've been trying to learn more about the bible ever since you helped me get into that private school. We got a religion class at school, but it's nothing like the Rap Session." Lucious thought that was odd because last month, he was the blame by Aaron, having to attend a parochial school.

Aaron was uninvited but still he managed to pull up a chair and joined Emmanuel and Lucious. Meanwhile, Lucious began to formulate what he thought was a brilliant idea; using the computer to look up Bible scriptures. "So, Aaron you can type in a subject or word and get scriptures that apply to it? Why didn't I think of that?" Emmanuel looked mystified; "I thought that was called the concordance in the Bible?" Aaron and Lucious looked intently at one another, thought about it for another second and ignored Emmanuel altogether. James walked over and greeted the trio. "Hey, Lou. You can relax now, I'm here." He said mockingly. James resembled Boris Kudjoe; he was young and single and he stood 6'9". He looked like he belonged on a basketball court instead of managing a restaurant. He often used his position as manager to wine and dine his female friends.

Despite the interruptions Lucious was focused, he knew he needed a plan of action. "Listen Aaron, I'm going to need you to help me tonight. Meet me at 6:30 instead of 7:00." He thought the best bet would be to do something a little different. As Aaron moved toward the exit, he exclaimed "Aight Lou. Yo, I'm gonna be a preacher." Aaron was always full of jokes so Lucious did not know when to take him seriously. Aaron continued "Do you know I can get a fully typed sermon on-line? And if I put my laptop on the podium I can act like I know the whole Bible. I'd tell the congregation to turn to about eight different scriptures and then after that I'd hit them with a short 'and the good Lord said' kind of sermon, unlike Pastor Money's long, screaming about nothing kind of sermons. I'd past the plate around three or four times and Cha-Ching I got that Gwop." "Got what?" Lucious asked while he attempted to quiet Aaron down. "That gwop, Lou. I'm sorry. Sir, please allow me to rephrase myself, while I collect large amounts of money." As Aaron got progressively louder the guests began to turn and look. "Lou, you like that idea? And on fourth Sunday's instead of what ya'll call Youth Sunday, I figure we spice it up and call it, Hip Hop Sunday. The choir will be full of video chics. Instead of singing Hymns, we switch it up and sing along to a rap song. And forget about wearing your Sunday best and wear school gear."

As Aaron tossed his coat over his back he abruptly asked, "Can I go now?" Lucious politely excused himself from Emanuel and escorted Aaron to the door. Once outside from the guests he said to Aaron, "You know what I once heard a movie star say during her acceptance speech, 'you'll be amazed by what you get, if you quietly, clearly and authoritatively demand it.' Since you work for me and if you would like to continue working for me, you are only allowed to ask two out of the three ways.

Listen. Never let another human being intimidate you, Aaron. If something is yours, then they do not have the power to take it from you, unless you give it to them." Aaron was apprehensive as he stood in the restaurant door while Lucious discretely returned to his seat and interviewed Emmanuel. Without losing his spot in the conversation and refocusing his attention to Emmanuel, he stated, "we have a Rap Session for teenagers at our church. We serve dinner and have a great, open conversation about subjects relating to the youth of today. You are more than welcomed to come if you'd like."

Emmanuel smiled. He appreciated the invite from Lucious, but first he had to know. "Do I have a job?" He asked. "Sure." Lucious laughed. "You had the job the moment you shook my hand. I will go over everything with you tomorrow, after school and you can fill out all the necessary paper work. How far do you live?" Lucious was surprised to find out that the young man lived around the corner from the restaurant and walking distance from his church. Terrance Avenue was directly in back of Lucious restaurant and was considered one of the worst neighborhoods on Long Island, with all the drugs, crime, "plain clothes" police officers, gangs and overcrowded streets. The streets were the children's playgrounds, while mothers cautiously watched in fear. Lucious on the other hand met individuals who had the same interest as anyone else in the town. There were people who wanted a safe neighborhood, clean parks and less drug trafficking. But this young man found the strength to defy the odds and exceed everyone's expectations while living on a block filled with many distractions.

Despite his accomplishments, Emanuel wished he could enjoy his adolescence like the affluent teenagers just one block over. There were million dollar homes on the very next block from whence Emmanuel lived. The homes were images out of a magazine, yet he and thousands of others lived in a one block radius, in packed apartments on Terrance Avenue. The people that stepped out of these million dollar homes would drive pass Emmanuel with a preconceived notion of who he was. It was amazing to Emmanuel how his block was patrolled by the police to contain his neighbors; while on the very next block his neighbors knew not to cross or they would most likely be detained. The teenagers from his projects walked passed drug addicts as they exited their doors. Emanuel often wondered if the *'over crowdedness'* of the projects indirectly led to the unacceptable social behavior that plagued his streets.

He was determined to show people not only who he was, but "whose" he was. The police knew he was different. They also took special notice to the young men; with undercover cops and surveillance cameras constantly on the block keeping track of what they considered "future criminals."

People often marveled at the wisdom of the young man and Lucious was no exception. The interview was long over but Lucious enjoyed getting to know Emmanuel's personal motivation. "I was always told that I have an old spirit." Emanuel responded as he read Lucious' expression. It was as if he was an angel brought here to help make a difference in others lives, but how could he, when he is so young? Emanuel serenely began to quote the Bible to Lucious,

Psalm 96:13 "He will come to judge the earth and he will judge our world on righteousness and people will be judged on truth"

"I told them last week in my article something God laid on my heart." "What did you preach about?" He laughed to himself as he realized he was speaking to a seventeen year old.

Luke 12:48 "From everyone who has been given much, much will be required of them; and to whom they entrusted much, of him they will ask all the more."

Emanuel continued. "I should have hatred in my heart but I refuse because hatred will only lead me to hell at an early age, with a heart attack. See, I say to people who have yet to do anything to inspire young people like me. The *Truth of the Matter* is: The enemy thanks them for not giving us the proper tools, equipment, training, skills or education to continue on in this struggle. They don't even give out Bibles. The enemy thanks them for giving up on me, but Jesus took me in. Thanks them for not showing me how and why I should vote. Thanks them for removing prayer from my school. Thank them for not eating healthy or eating together as a family on Sundays, but introducing me to fast food and causing me to deal with obesity, diabetes and heart related diseases at my age. Thanks everyone for taking a rest at the wheel. Thanks them for allowing my school to be misused and abused by unqualified people. Thanks them for not taking me in and not teaching me what they've been taught. The enemy especially thanks them for not taking me to church or teaching me the Bible." Lucious sat absorbing the message God sent through that child. He knew that great works would come through him.

Before letting Emmanuel leave, Lucious called and spoke with his mother, Mary, and confirmed what time her son was to meet him at the church. Her voice sounded groggy and hung over. She was more concerned about a job for herself than for her son, but she was very caring. Lucious thought about everything he knew about Emanuel. He remembered the article the young man wrote and thought about where he lived and went to school. Lucious wondered how all these things worked together to make the young Emanuel who he was.

Emmanuel left saying, "I will leave you with this question of the day. "Before a person acts upon anything, they should ask themselves one question. What would God do?"

Part Thirteen

Lucious rushed home to check with his wife and to give her dinner. He jumped in the shower to prepare for the evening. With water streaming down his face, he peered through its etched glass door. He gazed at his wife who was standing in the mirror in a silk nightgown. The roundness of her new belly made the fabric cling to her body. He admired her new body and it aroused him. He watched as she gradually oiled her skin. Sarah was radiant. She deliberately seduced Lucious as her baby brown eyes pulled his imagination closer. Her bright red pumps showed her freshly pedicure feet, as one of the straps from her silk nightgown fell perfectly from her shoulder. Lucious was like a deer caught in a car's headlights. He knew he should move but the blood had stopped moving upward to his brain and spiraled downward showing his manhood. As Franklin Brown's jazz CD filled the air, Lucious knew she was beckoning him.

Sarah's spontaneity hadn't changed. It was not a matter of waiting to be chased by her husband. The **truth of the matter** was she was a woman in need. She did not care how many hours Lucious worked in the restaurant. She was not concern with if he did not have any energy to have sex or if her stomach was too big for their sex life. If he had even attempt to look in the direction of another woman, he would fall asleep from exhaustion. Sarah sex drive during her pregnancy was in over drive, mean while Lucious walked around like a zombie. Lucious continuously wonder how his sex drive changed but was explained to by other men who had gone through similar situations during their wives pregnancies. He was told to hang in there a thousand times.

Lucious walked from the steamy shower into his pregnant wife's welcoming arms; indulging himself in what he saw as one of the perks of marriage. The beast was awakened but with a softening touch and aggressive demands from Sarah caused Lucious' to peak. Cautious not to harm his unborn child, Lucious tamed the beast and in that moment Lucious forgot about everything else and made love to his wife.

---

1 Corinthians, Chapter 7:1-9 Apostle Paul answers some cases proposed to him by the Corinthians about marriage. He shows them, marriage was appointed as a remedy against fornication, and therefore that persons had better marry than burn. He gives direction to those who are married to continue together, though they might have an unbelieving relationship.

Verse
1 "Now concerning the things where of ye wrote unto me: It is good for a man not to touch a woman (becoming perverted).

2 Nevertheless, to avoid fornication (booty-calls), let every man have his own wife, and let every woman have her own husband.

3 Let the husband render (give up the goodies) unto the wife due benevolence (willingly): and likewise also the wife unto the husband.

4 The wife has no power of her own body (sex), but the husband: and likewise also the husband has no power of his own body, but the wife.

5 Do not keep sex from you spouse, except it be with consent for a time, that ye may give yourselves to fasting and prayer; and come together again, because the devil will tempt you for holding back (sex).

6 Apostle Paul, continues, But I speak this by permission (by God), and not of commandment.

7 I wish all men were capable of being strong enough to sustain from sex, as I myself (but we are not). But every man has his proper gift of God (i.e. abstinence or self-discipline), one after this manner, and another after that.

8 I say therefore to the unmarried and widows, It is good for them if they tolerate even as I.

9 But if they cannot contain their sex drive, let them marry: for it is better to marry than to burn."

Lucious thought to himself and laughed. She entertained his mockery. "What?" She asked. "If this is our pre-anniversary, I can only wonder what we are in store for next week when we celebrate our one year anniversary." "And don't you forget," she said as she stood and disappeared into the bedroom.

After freshening up, Lucious jumped into baggy Marc Echo jeans and a designer G-Unit sweatshirt. He grabbed his Timberland's, his fitted baseball cap and black Roca-A-Wear leather jacket and glanced in the mirror as he headed out the door. Lucious quietly thanked his father for teaching him, at least, the appropriate time for casual and professional attire. His father was a terrible dad and worst as a husband but what he lacked, he surely made up the difference as a businessman. As a business owner, Lucious was disappointed in young people not wearing appropriate attire for an interview. He constantly found himself explaining, "When going to an interview for a job it calls for a business suit and not comfortable gear."

His excitement grew as he rushed to the Rap Session to teach that lesson. In five minutes he was walking through the doors of the U2CGS Mega Church.

"Call me a cheater but I brought my lap top to the church." Lucious said to God, as he headed in the church. Lucious kept a detailed outline of everything he and Deacon Taylor talked about. The plan was for each point he would turn to Aaron and say, "where in the bible can we look that up?" Aaron's role made him feel important.

Emmanuel attempted to enter the room unnoticed. His efforts were embittered as Lucious' church thugs gawked at his 3-piece suit. Aaron walked between Lucious and Emmanuel as they greeted one another. "Pastor Money has just entered the building." Aaron shouted as the class laughed hysterically. Lucious quickly asked Emmanuel to take a seat and insisted Aaron open the class with prayer. With a crack in his voice and perspiration forming on his forehead he nervously proceeded to pray. With a corporate "Amen" the class laughed at his meager prayer.

Lucious then chimed in with a special prayer for Deacon Taylor and blessed the food. They did not have enough food to go around. The class had doubled in size. Lucious was however, glad to see new faces. "For those of you who are new to this class, can you introduce yourselves to the rest of us?" They all looked around at one another. "Raise your hand if you are not a member of this church." Half the class raised their hands and the members began to shout out their guests names. Lucious quickly raised his voice, "One at a time. He knew everyone was excited about his or her friends but he requested that the guests speak for themselves. Lucious wanted them to feel comfortable about the topics in an open forum. "Let me say this, we do have rules. You need a Bible to follow along. If you do not have a Bible I will supply you with one. You need to respect other people when they are speaking. Young men, you will respect our young ladies and young ladies will act like ladies. You are more than welcome to bring anyone to our class; but only those in high school or college. Last but not least, the topics relate to you, but we want the topic to also relate to God. My task is to show you how what is going on today: drugs, gangs, music, etc., is actually addressed in the Bible and what the Bible has to say about it."

They went straight into the discussion. The topic was: Christmas with a twist: Love thy neighbor vs. Who are they? "Our text will come from:

James 2:8 "...they should love their neighbor as they love themselves."
Matthew 22:34-40, Galatians 5:13-14

"Do we all know why we celebrate Christmas?" Lucious asked the class, not sure if he had to explain Christmas or not. "We celebrate the birth of Jesus Christ. Every year on your birthday you receive gifts, right?" The class did not answer but wondered where he was going with the question. "You all expect to get something from the people who claim to love you the most and they better not disappoint you. Then tell me why on the day that is not your birthday; you have your hands out? We should be giving a gift to Jesus Christ not the other way around." The class was in an uproar. Some of the young people started yelling out statements. "Jesus wants us to share with one another," one person said.

Lucious had to reel the class back into the topic. He called on Emmanuel to explain in his own words what Christmas meant to him and what he thought about loving his neighbors. Emmanuel stood and spoke passionately about the meaning of Christmas. He projected his voice and spoke so eloquently that the class forgot he was their peer. They did not see him as one of them. He was a young kid dressed like an old man. "The Gospels according to Matthew and Luke both say that Jesus was born in Bethlehem. According to Luke, Joseph a carpenter and Mary a virgin were from Nazareth but had to travel to Bethlehem to be counted in a census ordered by Caesar Augustus. Jesus was born in a manger in Bethlehem during this trip. After Jesus' birth, the family fled to Egypt and then to Nazareth to escape a slaughter of baby boys in Bethlehem ordered by the Jewish king Herod.

I believe Christmas to be in my heart. Gifts came very few, for me and life has not been easy, so I believe Christmas is about sharing with the people you love, big or small. All I have ever had was my mother, I've prayed for a day when I would have family to rely on, but God supplies my every need. As God continues to give us gifts, we should give gifts to others. But not commercializing Jesus' birth. I think it is a shame how people who never step foot in a church, never worship God and do not have a relationship whatsoever with our Lord and Savior Jesus Christ, can taint the true meaning of Christmas. I have only spent Christmas with just my mom and me and as a child who came from the smallest family. I can remember not getting anything for some Christmas'. That is not important to me, but believing Jesus was born on this day, is." Emmanuel took a quick pause and hoped his peers would understand him as he continued. "I'm not Jesus but if I was him and I decided to return to earth on my own birthday, you'd better have a surprise birthday cake waiting and a gift."

Lucious jumped in and thanked Emmanuel. "It should not take an act of God for you to learn who you're neighbors are, either. I want us to do something real simple; I want you to get the address of three neighbors who live on your block. I purchased Christmas Cards and stamps. I want you to mail them a Christmas card." The young people looked around at one another questioning their assignment. "What if we do not know our neighbors' names or their house numbers?" Shemaiah asked. "Simply address them as, Dear Neighbor. As far as their addresses, just figure it out based on your address." Lucious said, "This will be the greatest gift and by the next class I want each of you to tell me how it went."

Lucious politely points at one of the guests, who happened to be sitting close to Shemaiah. "Shemaiah is he a friend or family member?" The young man sat quietly throughout the class. He wore a blue du-rag and blue fitted baseball cap that sat perfectly propped on his head, Airforce One sneakers, and white sweater with blue "Sean

John" letters printed boldly across the chest, Sean John jeans. He accentuated his gear with a fake platinum long chain with diamond encrusted but really "silver" pendant that swayed as he moved. "He's a very good friend of mine," Shemaiah replied with a devilish grin and a sultry voice. Their eyes met as they silently agreed to their relationship. Lucious looked intently as to study the couple in their church class setting.

As the class came to close, Lucious pulled Aaron to the side, "Aaron is Shemaiah and her friend involved in a gang or something?" Because of Aaron's involvement with gangs has made Lucious recognize the signs. Aaron laughed at Lucious' ignorance. "Where you've been? Our school is full of gangs. Let's just say, being in church is the only thing that kept us from trying to kill each other." Lucious looked sternly at Aaron, waiting for a simple yes or no. "Yes and no," Aaron replied. "What does that mean, yes and no?" Lucious asked in frustration. "She isn't but he's down," Aaron confesses. "Thank you for making it clear," Lucious said.

Lucious quickly changed the subject "whatever happened to the Spanish kid down the block from you?" Lucious knew that the kid had been locked up recently. He had thought long and hard about how to make things right between the two young men. The way Aaron dealt with the situation would affect the rest of his life. Lucious could only pray it would affect Aaron in a positive way. "I want you to send a Christmas card to the Spanish kid and I want you to put twenty dollars in the card." Aaron's eyes went up in the air, "he's locked down and for what? I don't know his address." Lucious took a quick look at Aaron, "figure it out but I'll give you until the next class. Remember, you have to work with me and you will reap what you sow."

Galatians 6:7 "Be not deceived. God is not mocked: For whatsoever a man sowed, that shall he also reap.

Job 4:8 it says, "Even as I have seen they that plow iniquity, and sow wickedness, reap the same."

Psalms 126:5 it says, "They that sow in tears shall reap in joy."

Luke 12:24 it says, "Consider the ravens: for they neither sows nor reaps; which neither has storehouse nor barn; and God feed them: how much more are ye better than the fowls?"

Part Fourteen

It was December 30th and everyone was preparing to bring in the New Year. Lucious and Sarah normally celebrated with friends. However, since Lucious opened his restaurant, they brought in the New Year with guests. They found themselves watching as customers celebrated around them. The days when the two of them traveled into New York City to watch the ball drop were long gone. Instead, they made the best of working that night and enjoyed each other's company.

That year Sarah wanted to do something different. She knew standing on her feet and serving guests all night would be too much of a challenge for her. Lucious was busy making final preparations. Lucious and his staff were expecting a full and crazy house. They had planned for a successful evening. He did not account for Sarah joining him that evening. Despite her small bulging belly, Sarah arrived ready to be put to work. She enjoyed the attention, the unusual kindness from strangers and the pampering from her husband.

"Hello Mrs. Bell," Aaron said. "Can I get you something?" The pampering had begun already. Sarah glowed; her smile was beaming and her stomach slightly protruding. Her clothing was very fashionable. Sarah was always conscious of how she looked because this placed great importance on how she felt throughout her pregnancy. It was not like her mother and the women before her; pregnancy was now a beautiful thing. A woman could wear clothes that were as comfortable but as appealing as a woman who was not carrying a baby. Celebrity women during their pregnancies were not hidden, but instead walked the red carpets. Sarah made other women proud when they would notice her feet. During her entire pregnancy she continued to wear her high heels. Four inch stilettos were normal. "Girl, how do you do it," one employee asked. "Beauty before pain," was how Sarah replied.

Lucious walked from his office to find his staff surrounding his wife. The restaurant was open, but very few came in before the holiday. He coughed to catch everyone's attention. His wife smiled as he walked in her direction. "What's up with the mother of my child?" Lucious asked as one of his cooks lay a huge plate of food in front of Sarah. He tried talking her out of her high heels, especially walking around the high school but she refused.

Lucious called Emmanuel over to meet Sarah, "Emmanuel, this is my wife Mrs. Bell." Emmanuel was elated because Mrs. Bell was his English teacher at Bishop Edgar A. Love High School. "I know Emmanuel very well." Sarah said as she greeted one of best students. Emmanuel walked away as Sarah began to feast. In an attempt to hide her hunger and continue to be a lady with class, he kept the conversation minimum as she ate and talked. "Do you know that kid will be a preacher one day? His heart is made of gold. He has been through so much but he never wears it on his shoulders. I only know because of a special program he is in at my school. But you would have never known if you were not told." Sarah remembered to inform Lucious of his mentor. "Before I forget, I hear Deacon Taylor is doing much better and will be released from the hospital real soon and Shemaiah's been coming to my class after school." Sarah took another huge bite of her food and began to talk with the food in her mouth, forgetting her rule to conduct herself as a lady at all times. *Oh! Please, for crying out lout, I'm pregnant.* She thought to herself. "What?" She asked Lucious, as he looked at her, funny. "Nothin," he quickly responded. "Look. I'm feeding for two and we're hungry." Lucious kept his comments to himself. "You were talking about Shemaiah." She was lost for a second as she swallowed the last bite of food from her plate. "Shemaiah comes to talk and trust me when I say that girl can talk." Sarah said while attempting to eat her dessert in front of Lucious. Lucious sat quietly as he wonders why his beautiful pregnant wife and mother-to-be decided to help in the restaurant. If he said anything she will deny it and blame him for asking. Until the great revelation Sarah worked in the restaurant begrudgingly with Lucious. The pregnancy allowed her to quit her part-time position in the restaurant and continue willingly with her other two full time positions as a school teacher and wife.

Lucious continued to look on waiting for Sarah to come forth and state why she was there. "Ooooh I telling you how your little church girl, Shemaiah and her so-called 'huzzband' came strolling in my after school class. That boy ain't but eighteen and got the nerve to address her to me as his wife-y." Lucious chuckled as Sarah tried to control herself. But the subject obviously hit a nerve and caused Sarah head and hands to move uncontrollably. Lucious intervened, "all of these young guys call their girlfriends their wife-y. It's no big deal. The ladies think it is alright." He realized by his last statement, he was implicated. He just said the wrong thing to a pregnant woman because she began to scold Lucious the same way she rebuked Shemaiah's so-called husband.

"First of all, it ain't cute. It's disrespectful to a woman. You are not going to call me wife-y and not give me a ring." Lucious nodded his head in agreement as Sarah continued to give her dissertation on the word wife-y. "A **wife-y** is defined as: A name given to young Black woman by a Brother in a false commitment of marriage; hoping to receive all the benefits of a husband without the responsibility to their wife. They are not officially married. The man is given all the perks of a marriage without God's covenant; could be a serious relationship; degrading to women. Need I go further?" Sarah said as her eyes popped out of her head and chill pumps rolled up her arms. Lucious was willing to debate his wife on this topic. But Sarah's emotions echoed through the restaurant and slowly women applauds broke her concentration. Lucious kept his thoughts to himself. Sarah looked away from Luscious as women passionately highly praised her for her stance on women's rights.

But Sarah was just getting warmed up when she stood from her seat and held on to Aaron as he assisted her from her chair. "My grandma use to say to the women in the family, 'why would a man buy the cow when he can get the milk for free?" Sarah looked Aaron in his eyes. Aaron looked Lucious in his eyes as if he was saying to Lucious, *man please save me from your crazy wife and the rest of these crazy women in here.* Sarah forcefully held on to Aaron's hand as she walked across the restaurant dragging him along the way. She caringly grabbed the hand of a strange young girl sitting with an older man; in Sarah's eyes was conspiring. She looked the young lady in the eyes as the rest of the restaurant rallied behind Sarah's words. "If you give him everything before you are married without a covenant from God then what will motivate him to walk you down the aisle, when he's already is playing house? The Bible says when a man findeth a wife, he findeth a good thing. So, don't allow NO man to call you **wife-y** until he can truly make you his wife. The young lady stood from her seat and started clapping as Sarah rolled her eyes at the man twice the young girl's age sitting looking at her in anger. The old man carefully evaluated the situation and did the manly thing. He got up and left. Aaron was forced to accompany Sarah as she strutted like Naomi Campbell, down the restaurant run way.

Ephesians 5:28 "So husbands ought to love their own wives as their own bodies; he who loves his wife

loves himself."   Women walked over to greet Sarah and to congratulate her on her pregnancy. The small crowd left Sarah and Lucious to be alone. Sarah, in a submissive way began to radically blink her eyes at Lucious as she drank from her class and removed the sweat off her face, as a preacher normally would do after giving an inspirational message to their congregation.

"Honey, do you have to work this New Year?" Lucious saw it coming and what better place for Sarah to ask than in public. They had been over this since he opened the business. "Our parents would like us to all go and my mother is picking me up if you are not able to drive me to the church." Sarah looked across the small dining table to see whether Lucious would bite at her request or ignore her completely.

Sarah found it difficult to understand her husband having to work twelve hour days, every weekend and on every holiday. She was very supportive, but there came a time when she fought long and hard for Lucious to take time out of the business and to go on vacation for a week.

"Can we spend this New Year in church?" Sarah muffled, with a mouth full. Lucious carefully looked at his wife. He felt like he was being asked to do something out of his reach. Without turning a question into a debate he quickly answered, "No." Sarah took a deep breath as Aaron refilled her glass of water. "Excuse me Mrs. Bell, but can you tell Lucious that I'm old enough to work a New Year's party? He has me off because I'm too young. My Mom said it was okay." Sarah smiled at Aaron as Emmanuel chimed in but she had promised to never get in between Lucious and the employees. She constantly found employees doing the mom and dad act when Lucious did not give them their way. "I will see what I can do," she said. Aaron walked away fussing at Emmanuel and how he ruined his chance to work on New Year's Eve.

Without further delay, Sarah quickly jumped back into the subject, "I don't think its right that we're working every New Year's Eve. We should spend it in church because we have too much to be thankful for. Plus, you have James to cover for you." Both Lucious and Sarah tried keeping their voices down but Lucious did not feel like this was the time or place. Sarah made one plea to Lucious, "I would like to go to church. Because of my pregnancy I can't work this year with you and I do not want to sit here all night talking to people." Lucious, asked his wife to be excused and rushed off but not before saying, "Let me know when you are finished and I will walk you to your car."

Part Fifteen

It was New Years Eve and Sarah and Lucious had little to say to one another, but she thought she would try to persuade him one last time. "Lucious are you sure you won't come to church with me tonight?" "I told you I have to be at the restaurant. Have a good night and tell our folks I said hello." He said with rage.

Franklin Brown's Live Band was rocking and the people were packed into the restaurant. It was less than two hours until the countdown and there was standing room only. Lucious and his staff created a small dance floor close to the band and it was packed people dancing. Everyone had eaten and Lucious took one last walk through the crowd, making sure to greet each one of his guests personally, before heading into his office to take a quick break away from all the excitement.

Just a few blocks away, the pews for the "Watch night" church service started to fill. Several stood patiently by the altar awaiting a chance to give their testimonies. The choir sang with renewed joy and the members welcomed one another wholeheartedly. Sarah waved to her mother-in-law, sitting just a few pews away, as she, her mother, her brother and his family settled into their seats.

A bellowing scream echoed from the dining room followed by a clamoring knock at Lucious' office door. He jumped up and almost knocked James, the night manager, over as he went to see what happened. The crowd was huddled over an older man lying motionless on the dance floor. "What happened?" Lucious demanded with a crack in his voice. "They think he had a heart attack," said James. "Everyone stay calm." Lucious said *frantically*. "James, has anyone called an ambulance?" "Yes, they're on the way."

The Holy Spirit filled the air at U2CGS. This service was like no other. The praise team danced down the isles as though they were floating on air. The elderly mothers of the church gave testimonies that pierced the hearts of the congregation. It was a heart felt celebration.

The EMT's rushed into the restaurant with a stretcher and began administering CPR as they transported him to the ambulance. "Where's this man's family?" Lucious asked James discretely. James did not speak. He pointed out of the window to an elderly lady being consoled by a younger woman. The two women walked away from the ambulance sobbing hysterically. As they climbed into their car the ambulance *silently* pulled away. The room was silent. Lucious asked the band to play something soft as the guests began to leave. "Please assist the rest of these guests James. I'll be in the kitchen."

The staff stood around in the kitchen waiting for Lucious' direction. Lucious knew that his demeanor would set the tone for his employees. "Do me a favor; let's try to make the best of the night." Emotions began to get the best of some of the waitresses. Lucious continued. "I would like us to say a quick word of prayer for that man and his family." James watched over the remaining guests in the dining room.

Lucious emotional prayer caused those who were holding back their tears to begin balling. The spirit was moving and the staff held one another as many of them had encountered life and death. "Somebody get James for me," Lucious requested. Lucious spoke to James as his staff listened. As he spoke, he wiped tears away that some of his staff saw as grief but to Lucious they were mixed emotions. "I'm leaving to go be with my wife. She's in church and I need to be with her. A man nearly died in my restaurant and all I can think of is my unborn child. I don't belong here right now; I belong next to my wife, so please excuse me as I follow my heart." Lucious walked out of the kitchen as his staff's clapped their hands in celebration of his love for his wife. "Go and get your wife and say a little prayer for all of us," one of his employees said as he was given the smile of an angel. "Do me a favor and take over for me," Lucious said to James and then disappeared.

Twenty minutes before the count down, Lucious sped down the street. His church was minutes away and the hardest part, would be finding a parking space at a packed church. He illegally parked his car with its hazardous light on. As he walked through the door of the church, Pastor Money was preaching. Lucious asked one of the elderly ushers, dressed in an all white nurse's uniform. Her well aged face was made up for the paparazzi to take pictures. Her purely gray hair was done to perfection. Her smile had a glow. She stood at the entrance into the sanctuary, welcoming guests. "Can you help me find my wife?" The elderly woman looked at Lucious with a frown on her face and in disgust for being disturbed while she listened to her Pastor preaching. He smiled childishly and Christian-like to keep the elderly usher, who turned into a security guard, from forbidding him from entering. Pastor Money was coming to a close, "you may now enter," she said while holding church programs, which could turn into a nightstick if he had acted up. He willingly followed the lead of the elderly church usher to an empty seat but then he spotted his wife.

As he began to walk over to where she was seated with her family, the elderly church usher nodded her head and militantly turned around and walked back to her post. Pastor Money asked the church to come forward and close to the altar. Sarah turned around to see Lucious at her side, standing at the altar. She could not help the smile that said a thousand words, "what are you doing here?" She asked quietly as Lucious' eyes filled up with tears. "Long story," he replied.

Lucious turned to see his mother from a distance. Everyone was anticipating the count down in the next two minutes. Pastor Money was on "fire" and the congregation was full of happiness. Lucious laughed as Aaron graciously made his way through the crowd to stand in between he and his wife. "Ha, Mr. and Mrs. Bell," Aaron said with a childish smirk.

"Ten, nine, eight, seven, six, five, four, three, two, one," the congregation yelled. "HAPPY NEW YEAR," they roared as they embraced one another. Lucious, his wife and Aaron headed back to their seats. Lucious spotted Abraham, Deacon Taylor's son. Abraham placed a thumb in the air, to indicate to Lucious, his father was all right. Lucious, gestured a small salute back in his direction. Lucious knew God was a miracle worker when he looked down and saw Deacon Taylor sitting in his wheelchair next to Abraham. *What a God we served*, Lucious told himself as he smiled walking back to the pew where Sarah was sitting.

"Start your new year off with giving to the Lord," said Pastor Money. He projected his voice anticipating a great harvest as he stared out into the packed congregation. His bright striped, red suit and white shoes helped his audience enthusiastically participate in the service. "Place your offering in the basket," Pastor Money loudly said into the microphone.

Part Sixteen

Lucious decided to check on Deacon Taylor. Deacon Taylor's house was one of the few homes that were well maintained and his landscaping was impeccable. His home looked like a home out of a southern style magazine. His property if it were not for the neighboring homes could go well over half a million. Deacon Taylor like so many of his friends were notorious for having some of the biggest and most lavish homes on the Island but throughout the years with the spike in taxes, crime, influx of rental homes and bad press had turned one of the best neighborhoods into the worst place to live on Long Island. Those that were fortunate to inherit such properties found it difficult to maintain these homes and either ran them into the ground or out right foreclosed.

Lucious and Aaron could hear the television coming from Deacon Taylor's house as they walked up to the door. Deacon Taylor's assistant opened the door expecting their company. The moment he and Aaron stepped foot in Deacon Taylor's immaculate house, his assistant told them, "Deacon Taylor will be with you in a second." Lucious walked around the living room studying all the pictures that encrusted the wall with memories; while Aaron sat like a statue. Lucious could not help notice the transformation in Abraham's life as he saw another person in all the pictures. Aaron saw trophies, plaques, which adorned a grand piano; used to decorate it with accolades of Deacon Taylor's accomplishments in sports and as a leader in the community.

Rebecca Stanton, the news reporter voice projected from the television at full volume in Deacon Taylor's den. "After following the trials of the two alleged, GANG KILLERS for months. The cases on these two murders are closed. What's next for these gangsters? Because of their age, the trails have been kept under wrap and the juries have been practically held hostage in a near by hotel for two weeks. One member of the jury was so happy the trial was over that I was told her and her family has taken a long vacation. As you all may know. This trial is a federal crime because the deaths that have been committed by these teenager murders across state lines. Their sentence will be issue by the judge by Monday. We are being told by reliable sources allegedly that these gang members will be given the death sentence, in North Carolina. They are both seventeen.

Truth Of The Matter

In the past decade we have seen across America, teenagers being tried as adults. This is the first in American history, where a teenager is tried, convicted and executed for committing a crime. If they are allegedly convicted as adults, these teenagers will be given the stiffest penalty, death by injection. This is Rebecca Stanton, reporting live from Durham, North Carolina. The T.V. was turned off.

Deacon Taylor's assistant rolled him into the room. He snuck up on Lucious as he questioned Abraham's failure. He wondered what Deacon Taylor did wrong in raising his son? *Where did Abraham go wrong?* With a weak voice Deacon Taylor spoke as Lucious' back was facing him. Lucious leaped. "He is a great son, as both my children were but he allowed the worst to take hold of his life and put him in a place he could not escape. **Truth of the Matter** is: The hardest thing you can ever face in life is not being able to save your child. He was the most successful of him and his brother but his success was more important than God. My other son had God first and they both faced challenges, as we all do, but you need faith and God."

Deacon Taylor asked to be rolled over to the baby grand piano that sat in the middle of the room. He picked up a trophy that Abraham won as a child, as he sat beside Aaron. "You can only teach your children who God is but you can't save them. Your children will know one day that if you can't save them here on earth, imagine when you are standing at the gate and hoping God will allow your child into heaven. I got to the point in life, some years ago where I realized God could only save my son." Deacon Taylor seemed as though his days of lost sleep made him immune and numb.

"I forgave my son for excessive drinking and drug life. I forgave him when he drove a car drunk with his young family inside and they died because of his carelessness. I forgave him for causing that grief after we buried his older brother from A.I.D.S. But it took me a long time to forgive him when my wife died. She took all of it so hard. She went to sleep and never saw another day on earth. I love my son and I see him changing but I can not judge the changes in his life."

Deacon Taylor shifted the conversation to something a little more pleasurable. He said to Lucious with sincerity, "You will be a father soon. Cherish the time you spend with your child. Because you will judge yourself on the successes of your children but children will evaluate their father's based upon their hearts and their actions. God will judge everything about you." He looked over at Aaron, who appeared to be soaking up everything. "Young man, you have to think before you act on anything. The stakes are high and the penalty is costly. One wrong decision could cost you everything. I know you young people have a whole lot of choices to choose from and are free to do as you please in life but at what price? If you had my wisdom and I had your youth, we would be a great team and we can be. I want you to walk with Christ and be a leader. Do what will give God the glory and watch your life prosper abundantly."

Lucious had so much to tell Deacon Taylor about the class, but so much with so little time. Deacon Taylor was recovering and as much as Lucious wanted him to know, when the time came they would discuss all God's success in the ministry. They shock hands but before Lucious and Aaron parted, Deacon Taylor called their names, "Lucious, Aaron." Lucious turned as one foot was out the door. With a plea from Deacon Taylor, "I know it is hard and I know running a business and having a child on the way is not easy for a young man like you but don't give up. Stay in prayer and take care of Aaron and the rest of those children in the church; and send my love to your lovely wife."

Aaron smiled from being in the presence of two great men. "Deacon Taylor, you are very wise?" Aaron said as if he just received some sort of revelation but with sincerity. Deacon Taylor smirked, "Remember, young man, a still creek runs deep." Aaron looked over at Lucious for clarity. "Don't judge a book by its cover," Lucious interpreted.

Part Seventeen

Lucious was thrilled about the Rap Session coming up. The young people sent out Christmas cards. He wanted to know the result of what would happen when you gave an expensive gift with thoughtfulness and consideration to a stranger? The evening of the Rap Session, Lucious walked into the classroom with Aaron to find Pastor Money sitting in the room holding a conversation with Emmanuel. Lucious greeted his Pastor and Emmanuel, "Hello and what do we owe the honor of this visit, Pastor?" Pastor Money sat with a body language, which said, "He was unsure." He was surprisingly short on words but he stayed the entire class.

The young people began to pour into the room. Lucious' staff from the restaurant set up the food. Lucious quickly prayed for a miracle because he knew the class could get a little rowdy, especially depending on the subject. But as much as he was alert, so was the class. As Pastor Money looked on, the class prayed cheerfully, ate quietly, addressed the rules peacefully and respectfully introduced themselves.

The class had grown so much that Lucious had to ask Pastor to move them to another room. "Do you normally have this many young people?" Pastor Money asked Lucious, as they moved to another room. "No. But the class has grown in the past months. We are looking at about thirty- something young people in this room." As the class settled into their seats, Lucious asked, "how did everyone do with the Christmas cards you all mailed out to your neighbors?" Lucious explained the assignment to the visitors and with enthusiasm the class began to rave about their encounters. Lucious went around the room to find out the feedback; but what they just pulled off was the most heart felt thing any of them probably had seen in their young lives. "Isaiah screamed out of turn, "I want to do this again, because all three of my neighbors gave me a card with money in them." Lucious reminded the class, "The purpose was not to get money but getting to know your neighbors."

"My neighbors gave me gifts," one young person replied. Another person said how meeting her neighbor caused her family to meet a long distant relative. The door opened an hour into the class; Trustee Jordan disingenuously apologized for interrupting the class. The class speculated about who the people Trustee Jordan paraded into the class were before she had a chance to introduce them. They looked at Lucious for a hint but he too was not sure where Trustee Jordan was going with her guests. One of the rules to their class was, no adults or parents were allowed in the room to help let the young people speak freely but Trustee Jordan was introducing a mother and her son.

In Trustee Jordan's flamboyant way, "Pastor Money, Brother Bell and all of you young people, I do apologize but it gives me great pleasure to introduce to our church family a young man and his mother that Aaron has befriended." The class turned their attention to Aaron, who kept his eyes glued on his acclaimed friend. "What does befriend mean?" Isaiah whispered to another but loud enough for the whole class to hear. "His name is José and he used to go to school with my son. José is from El Salvador. He lives with Maria, his mother; Teresa, his older sister and Juan, his younger brother. Aaron and José had had some problems or "beef" as you young people call it, in school. Aaron sent some correspondence to a place José was staying." Without putting José's business completely out there and not confessing her only child is part of a gang, for all she knew, she omitted some of the details of the introduction to the class. Trustee Jordan placed Aaron on the spot and unaware of this intrusion, he followed his mothers lead "Aaron, I want you come up here and tell your class what you did."

"Can we get the edited version," Isaiah asked. Aaron made his way to the front of the room with his guard up from an old rivalry. He stood on the opposite side of the room not underestimating José, a person he considered an enemy. Aaron and José's body language told their story.

Aaron explained to the class, "Mr. Bell asked us to send out Christmas cards to our neighbors. José and his people live down the block from me. *Me and him* always had 'beef' because we were in different gangs around the way. I'm no longer gang bangin' but Mr. Bell had asked me to send him, José a card and some money. He was doin' time in the county. So, I sent him a few dollars and a card." Aaron looked over at José who felt appreciative. The class looked at Aaron not surprised he was in a gang but surprised he was giving up something they saw as a part of him.

Pastor Money stood from his chair. Lucious, not wanting the momentum to go away intervened, "Aaron, what's next and are you still in a gang?" Pastor Money started walking slowly to the front of room as he began to see a revelation take place amongst these young people. "I'm out of the gang business. I'm trying to do the right thing.

I don't want to die for something stupid. I want to own a business like you," He looked at Lucious. "I want to lead people like Pastor Money and I want my mother to see me graduate from college and watch me marry a fine woman. Life is too short for 'beefing' with people we hardly know. I have no problem with José. I want to be a better Christian. If I have to cut off all ties with some of the people I know, then oh! Well."

Trustee Jordan could only cry as she tried holding back her tears of joy. The young ladies in the class wiped their tears. The young men played tough. Shemaiah could not hide her emotion.

Lucious continued as if he was the host, "José what about you? Are you still with your gang or do you feel like that is all you have?" After listening to Aaron, José came clean. In a heavy Spanish speaking accent José began to tell his side of the story, "Mrs. Jordan asked me to be here, tonight. I was ready to kill this man," José said with conviction, while he looked in Aaron's direction. "But while I was locked up, this older Latino amigo who is a Christian told me something I never heard. He said my mother was home crying but Jesus wept even more for my soul. I took him as my amigo and he would read the Bible every day with me. My mother worked three jobs sometimes four, so we never had time for church and when my Poppy disappeared we never had time for each other, so I found my family in the streets." José paused for a second as he could feel his mother's pain without looking at her and then he continued, "I'm part of a gang." He reframed from throwing up any signs in the church.

He further said, "Aaron sent me that card; I did not know what to think." José looked over at his mother to see her cuddle with his sister and full of tears. "I asked my mother to go to his home and she said his mother was nice to her. Mrs. Jordan came to mi "familia's" house for Christmas and had dinner with mi "familia" and that meant a lot to them. Aaron is okay. I have no problem with him." They both shook hands.

Pastor Money at a snail's pace made his way to the front of the room. He stood beside José unafraid and moved by what the young Hispanic had to say. Pastor Money whispered to Lucious, "Are they members of our church?" Lucious shook his head, indicating "No" as his answer. "Do you normally take up a collection in this forum from everyone?" Lucious looked his Pastor in the eyes and this time answered him verbally, "NO."

Pastor Money added a few words before Lucious ended the class. As the family of José stood, Pastor Money's exhilarating voice moved the young people with a clear message and a way of inviting José. The **Truth of the Matter** is: "Latinos are our neighbors throughout America, so I can not complain about Latinos in "our" community because they support each other." Pastor Money chuckled as he continued to make a point. "They stand by one another and they clearly understand who their "enemies" are. We fight each other and then try to understand why our children are killing each other. If you've lived on this earth as long as I have, you'll know hate is taught. Why are we teaching young people to hate one another? All that we have been through and become, why are we still struggling and the Latinos are advancing? They work to achieve a better life and here you have a better life and don't work to keep it. I'm not mad at them but I'm mad at you, young people, because Latinos fight today, the way I use to when I was your age for the things you enjoy the most.

You young African-American and Hispanic people cannot be fooled to hate each other. Ask yourself why this country is making such a big deal over immigration today. Why are they paying billions of dollars to build a fence on one side of America but leave the other side wide open? Do you think they are pushing immigration laws on people from European countries? Wake up, young people. The jobs are no longer in America and the *jobless Americans* need somebody to blame. This country is as much mine as it is for any other person. This country was built on the blood of immigrants. Don't be a fooled." He went on to speak, as he looked each one of the family members in their faces. They looked back at him, not sure if they were welcome or in the wrong place at the wrong time. "José and his family are welcome here at U2 Can Get Saved." All in attendance gave a resounding round of applause.

Lucious concluded the class by stating, "If a person is not a member of your church, civic organization or even part of the same gang as you, you probably would not even realize that you are all neighbors. Why is that? It should not take an act of God for you all to recognize one another's existence. As young people in this class, you can only learn how to love your neighbor if you first introduce yourselves. Stop waiting for a formal introduction and open your mouths and introduce yourself to your neighbors."

Part Eighteen

Palm Sunday was the following week and Sarah was out of school for the next week. Her stomach was enormous and her nose was pudgy; still Sarah would strut around in her four inch stilettos. Her doctor left her alone about her high heels, but Sarah was disappointed when she was told by her OB-GYN, "No perms during her pregnancy." She tried explaining to Lucious the situation and how NO perm was a huge change for a Black woman to get use to but it went over his head.

Lucious was watching the WIRE, an HBO show about Baltimore, Maryland's hood, drugs, church, politics and young people of color and their unfortunate lifestyles. "Lucious can you pay attention to me for a second. You record every episode," she said as she held on to a magazine with the picture of her new look. Sarah without a second was ready to go from Tyra Banks weaved hairstyle that was long and straight. It gave her more of a glamorous look. But she was ready to wear a Halle Berry short cut that said adventurous and sassy. "I'm happy with whatever you're happy with, Baby," He said to Sarah, as he kept glued to the fourth season. Sarah threw the magazine on the table and decided to surprise her husband with her new look.

That afternoon Sarah decided to go to the hairdresser and get the shortest hair cut she ever had. The look was low maintenance, but she looked like a million dollars. When Sarah returned home, Lucious was shocked. He did not think she would actually do it. She said, "So, what do you think?" He thought she looked great no matter what. What he did not know was his next choice of words would have a bigger impact than he could ever imagine. "It looks OK, but it's too short." Sarah was silent. Lucious knew that meant trouble. She looked into the mirror to convince herself, she made the right choice.

Dr. Money, Pastor Money's wife was Sarah's most esteemed mentor. She was the first lady and a woman who exuded beauty, power, strength, humility, spirituality, and self confidence and submission to her husband/pastor. She was truly the opposite of her husband but they were made for one another. She was reserved, conservative and private. Pastor Money was outspoken, loud, always in the front, demanded attention and gave you his opinion whether you wanted or insist not to receive it. She was graceful in her maturity; and challenged the beauty and style of women half her age. She never raised her voice and her temper was modest; but she was the women not even the most powerful men of the town would reckon with. Her reputation far preceded her and Sarah admired all of this about her.

Many women attending the same church understood their Pastor' wife's role and the high demand of her time by other women who seek her friendship and listening ear. Sarah saw her as a hip-grandmother. Dr. Money dressed in her crimson fur-like shawl, red gloves and an ostentatious Swarovski pendant, smiled as she gave a sign of approval to Sarah. She clutched a ruby red purse that matched her church suit and hat. Her mocha skin may have had some surgery years ago but it now appeared flawless. Born, raised and educated in the south. Dr. Money learned the value of education and always drove for perfection. She pronounced every word with clarity and distinction. Dr. Money worked hard and when she had retired from the University rewarded herself with a vintage cherry red, sport Mercedes Benz.

Abraham rolled Deacon Taylor over to Sarah after an exhilarating Sunday church service. Lucious assisted Sarah into the lobby of the grand church, while she rubbed her stomach. As Sarah greeted Deacon Taylor, a voice spoke, "Good afternoon my Dear." Sarah turned away from her husband and in the direction of the unfamiliar voice coming from behind. The voice of Dr. Money startled Sarah because she spoke few words to those on the outside of her circle. Looking into the window some might consider her a Queen speaking to a peasant. The way she carried herself, the position and the responsibility as the first lady of a mega church and the enormous amount of pressure she had to help the Man of God save souls. "Hello Dr. Taylor and Abraham," Dr. Money acknowledged both men as she placed her hand on Sarah's stomach. "When are you due, my child? You look like you're ready to go in, any minute, Honey." Sarah was ready to have the baby today if God gave her a choice, "Not soon enough," she said with a very toothy grin. "I'm due in June," She admitted. "My Dear, do you know what you are having?"

Dr. Money asked Sarah while looking into the eyes of Lucious, looking for his reaction. "No. My husband and I have decided to torture ourselves with suspense. We don't want to know; all we want is a healthy child." Dr. Money was already impressed by Sarah. She thought her answer was old fashioned, but charming. "It's as if young people want answers right now. If God wanted you to know everything before it happened, where would He fit in?"

Both women smiled as they looked at the men who were watching them bond. Dr. Money grabbed the hands of Lucious as Pastor Money walked over, "I have heard so much about this young man." Lucious beamed as the attention was placed on him. "Continue to do the work of the Lord," said Pastor Money as he attempted to pull his wife away from her long conversation.

"Dr. Money! She has to be the classiest, old lady. She almost reminds, you of Diane Carroll," Lucious said to Sarah as he walked her to their Ford Explorer. Lucious assisted his wife into the truck without as much as a "thank you." The show (nice wife act) was over but Sarah was far from over with yesterday's issue. She felt like her concerns were neglected. Lucious was not about to bring the subject up. He knew Sarah was troubled, with what was a simple answer. When Lucious told his wife about her new hair style, "it looks OK but it's too short." During service, she made sure their bodies never touched. *What happened to the spirit of the Lord or the beautiful chemistry between her and Dr. Money? When did that pregnant glow disappear?* Lucious could only think to himself. "Are we still going to the movies tonight," Lucious had asked Sarah. She continued to ignore Lucious. He attempted to turn on some music; out came Kirk Franklin. In less then a second, Sarah turned the radio off before Kirk Franklin could go into the chorus.

"You owe me an apology," Sarah said as tears flowed down her face like a stream. "You had the audacity to say that to me," she said as her voice got louder and cracked while she spoke. Lucious understood that by giving "HIS" opinion to a pregnant woman was obviously wrong. "You asked me what I thought about your hair style; I gave you my honest opinion. What did you want me to say?" Lucious asked with a dumb-founded expression. "You think I'm unattractive and over- weight; even Dr. Money looks better than me and she's old enough to be my grandmother." Sarah shouted at Lucious. Lucious was reluctant to respond but went on the defense, "I have never said you were fat."

Lucious was inexperienced when it came to understanding a pregnant woman's emotional side. But was about to get a class, 101 Emotions Gone Wild. "Why haven't we..."? Sarah said, as she looked him straight in his face as he continued to drive. Lucious began to stutter as he tried explaining and driving, causing them to speed faster in their truck. "Is this because I said, your hair was too short?"

He asked. "I can care less what you think about my hair, when I asked you, you were busy watching TV. You had your chance." She said as her voice screeched and the pain roared from her body like a wounded lioness. "When was the last time...."? She bawled out. Lucious attempted to think. He had no good reason but he tried to explain,

"I have no excuse, Sarah. You know I've been busy with the business." He declared in a low voice. Like a solider that has surrendered, he held her hand and did his best to take blame for her hurt. "I'm sorry. I have no excuse." He began to sob as his wife cried in silence. "I love you and I would never do anything to make you think differently. Sarah, you know me." He pleaded.

"I refuse to be made to feel this way. I love you but I can't be the only person in this relationship and I will not carry this child alone. Lucious I need you. We need you," Sarah said as she continued to wail. "Lucious." She screamed as a mob of young people dashed across the street in gang paraphernalia. A car appeared out of nowhere, as Lucious steered the truck away from the mob of belligerent teenagers racing across the street. Lucious struggled to drive away from what materialized from nowhere. He attempted to hold his wife back with one hand from harm. Everything happened so suddenly.

"Sarah!" He yelled as he lifted his head. "Sarah!" He bellowed as he moved in her direction. "Sarah, talk to me." He said as her body swayed in his direction, motionless. "Sarah, don't move, stay still." He cried out, hoping she would respond. Lucious tried to make note of his surroundings but all he could see was his wife, lying still in the passenger seat and upside down. He was rescued from his vehicle but his helpless wife sat powerless and incoherent. Lucious became erratic. In his head he remained calm but no one was moving fast enough. The same young people who darted in front of his truck are curiously standing around as by-standers. Lucious began to hyperventilate as people rushed to help him remove Sarah from the truck, with no success.

The sounds of sirens were moving closer and closer. Lucious was shoved out of the way as his wife's body is hauled from the wreckage. He sat off on the curb rambling to himself as one EMT tried to comprehend. *I'm here. Jesus is here, now. The day has come. Jesus has returned. He has come to get you and me. The end is here. I understand what she explained about the Rapture. I see. I want her to know that I know. I studied it. She has to know that I know. How will she know that I know? How will she know that I love her if she leaves me?* He is escorted away from the ambulance, as the EMT's try everything to keep his wife and child alive.

His mind was going in every direction. The accident stopped traffic for miles. By-standers were silently watching as every move made by the EMT's, fire department and police officers were mentally recorded by the crowd full of strangers. "Sir, it would be best if we followed the ambulance in my car," The cop said to Lucious. Luscious who had squatted on the ground, looked up at the police office in silence. "Sir, we can follow your wife to the hospital in my car," The officer repeated. Luscious pushed the officer off of him as he was given a helping hand. The officer took it as nothing but hurt and grief, and then directed Lucious to his police car.

Part Nineteen

Aaron drove down the block to José's house. "This girl who lives in Westbury is giving a house party. You wanna go?" Aaron asked while they are both glancing over at José's mother. Aaron stood in the doorway. "Hello, Mrs. Lopez," Aaron yelled out with a voice assuring her. "Your mother knows where you're going?" Mrs. Lopez asked as she walked over to Aaron. "Yeahhhhh," He replied with the biggest smirk on his face. "Do you think she would let me drive the Benz if she didn't know where I was going?" He gave Mrs. Lopez his baby look but Mrs. Lopez still casing out the situation for any holes in Aaron's story. While José was busy taking his time getting dress, Mrs. Lopez continued to drill Aaron. "Be careful driving outside of this town because a Hispanic and African-American together in a Mercedes are asking for trouble." She said as she glanced out the door at the car Aaron was driving.

Aaron wanted José to hurry up before José's mother talked him out of going by planting all the fear in his heart for wanting to have a little fun. "If something was to happen, how we will know," Mrs. Lopez continued to ask. Aaron bent the truth but his half of a truth laid Mrs. Lopez's mind to rest. "You see that car out there? It has a navigational system that cannot only give you directions but it can track the whereabouts' of the car. The system can tell by its program if a stranger is in the car, by their weight in the seats, their voice and their body heat. The car has been programmed to call my mother's phone if it should go twenty-five miles from my mother's house." Aaron held his mother's key and remote starter in his hand. "A push of this panic button sends a signal to the closest police department. José was finally dressed.

Both Aaron and José leaped into Aaron's 5oo series Mercedes-Benz. "What took you so long," Aaron asked. As they sped down the block uprooting the dead by blasting the latest reggae tone of Daddy Yankee and collaborated hip-hop gospel music. "So where this girl live in Westbury?" José asked. "She lives off Post Ave.," replied Aaron. The music was as loud as the speakers could go. As they were coming off the highway and onto Post Avenue, Aaron spotted from his rear view mirror a police car trailing behind with the lights flashing.

"Yo! Bro. I don't like Five-0." José got awkwardly nervous. Aaron turned the music, down and quietly from reggae tone to his mother's gospel CD, one of Shirley Cesar's songs. Both teenagers sat still while two police officers walked up on opposite sides of the car. "License and registration," an African-American cop requested of Aaron. The Caucasian officer kept his eyes on José. "Where you headed?" The cop resembling Andrew Dice Clay asked José as he anxiously answered. "Ah, to his friend, I meant, our friends house." The African-American officer walked back over to Aaron's side of the window after looking for any warrants. "Whose vehicle is this?" He asked. Aaron became infuriated by all the questions and was not intimidated by either officer but José on the other hand started to sweat.

"I need you both to step out of the car," demanded the African-American officer. "José and Aaron slowly removed themselves from the car as traffic began to slow down and cop cars near by swarm in. The amount of cop cars that arrive caused a spectacle. You would have thought they caught a bank robber. "Officer what did we do?" Aaron yelled out as he is ignored. The African-American officer told Aaron his information as if he needed to be aware, "This is your mother's car. The car is registered in Marilynn Jordan's name, but I'm willing to let you go with a warning for speeding." Aaron looked at the officer with a question mark, not sure of the speed zone. He did not think he could have been driving fast with all the cars he was following. As Aaron tried to find out how fast he should have went, José jumped back into his seat.

The African-American officer passed Aaron a business card. José continued to look forward while in the passenger seat, not giving any eye contact to the officer, staying calm and speaking only when spoken to. Aaron slipped the business card to José without reading it. The front of the card read, Alex Bailey, Nassau County Police Officer. The back of the business card Officer Alex Bailey hand wrote, God Bless you and your family, Brother Alex, to Trustee Jordan.

As they drove up to the house, they were being followed by the same Nassau County's cops. The crowd outside the house indicated to them a booming party. Aaron parked his mother's Mercedes down the block from the house. They walked up the sidewalk. They were being eye- balled by a group of young men trying to assert power. It was like a lion placing it scent, trying to show control over a territory. Aaron and José pushed out their chests and confidently marched through the core of the crowd of strangers. As they swaggered past the crowd, a young lady sauntered over to Aaron with an Apple Bottom pair of denim jeans that provocatively caressed her buttocks. She wore a shirt barely covering her body, with a visible, pierced belly button.

José was not blind to his surroundings. He saw some people he considered as an enemy. Everyone wore the saying color, red. He was on the wrong territory. He played it cool and kept his guard up until a person whose face was covered with a red handkerchief bumped him. José would have normally said something in defense but he was out numbered. His days of gang bangin' was over. With a peaceful tone in his voice and his eyes facing toward the ground, "excuse me," he quickly said to the person rudely brushing pass him. "Who you 'rep,'" asked the roughneck with his dark eyes only appearing to the public. "Nobody. I represent nobody," José responded. Both the stranger and José kept it moving. A couple hours later, the stranger with the handkerchief and three others revisited José. He looked around for Aaron but Aaron was tied up.

The night was still early but José was ready to leave as anger registered in his eyebrows and his tone of voice had rage. Aaron wrapped around his girlfriend and threw his keys in José's direction. "I am right behind you," Aaron hollered as he tried to talk over the speakers blasting 50 cent, "I run New York" song. He made gestures at José, while he stood behind the young lady. José waved his hand in the air and walked out the door. Minutes later Aaron was walking out the door. "Walk It Out," single was deafening from the sound system and every young person was doing the latest dance from the "dirty south." Gunshots ring off, the crowd scattered and the house was jammed with frighten young people. The cops who turned the corner, made a u-turn back in the direction of the house. Sirens and cries replace the gunshots seconds later.

Aaron is face down on the ground. He slowly pulled himself up from the dirt and brushed himself off, his girlfriend ran out of the house and over in his direction, trembling with horror. "Where's José?" He shouted. She was not sure and fear embraced his every worst thought, as seconds turn into minutes. Police cars and the crowd of young partygoers surround Aaron's mother's car. Aaron thrust past the mob. What Aaron feared and what he prayed not to have happen was a reality; José was lying in a pool of blood.

Part Twenty

Lucious was distraught as family and friends tried their best to hold it together for his sake and their own. No one knew what was going on with Sarah's condition. The entire family huddled in small circles for encouragement and prayer. Lucious stood off on his own, trying to put all of this together. Silently he prayed and thought optimistically about his wife and his unborn child. He took another second and suddenly charged after the exit of the hospital. His mother ran after him.

The rain was beating down on her face. As raindrops lightly tapped on his face, he opened his eyes and ogled for a minute into the cloudy skies. His mother walked up and stood behind her son, giving him a moment. Lucious roared out every emotion knotting in his stomach, so the world could recognize his pain. "How could this have happened?" He asked rhetorically to his mother. "It was my fault. If I had made her happy, we would not have been arguing. I didn't make her happy."

Lucious howled as his mother tried to keep him from losing his composure. "Ma, we were coming from church. No. God wouldn't let this happen." Lucious sobbed loudly as patients and the hospital staff walked around him as he blocked the slippery entrance to the emergency room.

Just then Sarah's older brother raced up to Lucious' mother. He was out of breath and slopped over as he tried to gasp little air to his lungs. The family never thought this day of terror would grip the last ounce of breath from their bodies. Sarah's older brother and the way he repeatedly disregarded the doctor's recommendations as he dealt with being over weight, constantly short of breath, diabetic, high blood pressure and high cholesterol was the family's major concern. He tried gathering his breath as he arrived with an attempt to control his emotions and voice. "The doctor has news for the family." They gathered up Lucious and hurried themselves back into the building. He could hear Sarah's mother hollering before the elevator stopped. Just as the elevator came to a halt on the second floor; Lucious' heart dropped even lower as he walked up to the entire family. The family went from being as strong as a bear to as weak as a cub without its mother. Every eye was placed on him, fear cradled his body and Lucious did not take another step in their family's direction. The ***Truth of the Matter*** was not what he had wished to hear. He could not bear the truth. The long faces and tears gripped his body tightly. He could not breathe. He looked his mother in her eyes and flew down the stairwell of the hospital.

Part Twenty-One

The door bell rang, unexpectedly. Deacon Taylor looked up from the chair he sat in and asked his assistant, "Who could it possibly be?" He continued to study the Bible and listen to James Cleveland, a legendary gospel singer. He comfortably adjusted his position as he barely heard a voice other than his assistant in the house. Without flinching or removing himself from the "Word", his assistant walked into his room. The assistant, for a minute was mystified. He was lost for words as he stared in the direction of Deacon Taylor. Deacon Taylor looked up from his Bible into the face of a puzzled person and was uncertain why his assistant looked so perplexed. "Who was it? Is everything okay?" He waited for a response, while taking off his reading glasses, closing his Bible and adjusting his hearing aide.

In a cheerless and mind-boggling voice the assistant answered Deacon Taylor as his mind marveled at what he was about to relay. "There is a woman here who said she would like for you to meet your grandson."

Deacon Taylor's two grandchildren died years ago in a car accident caused by his drunken son, Abraham. His oldest son never had children before passing away from AIDS. According to Deacon Taylor, there are no grandchildren and this has to be some kind of mistake. Without another word and with the touch of a button Deacon Taylor began to rise from his antique motorized lift chair. His assistant quickly ran over to help. Deacon Taylor grabbed his Bible and gingerly moved to his wheel chair.

She dressed in what she considered her best. She was attempting to not look desperate or hopeless. She had a southern "twang". Although her manners were lady like she looked as though she fought a few wars and lost. She showed signs of a struggling woman. She wore her strife in her face and teeth. She was a survivor and did whatever it took to get by. But she quickly made herself clear. She was not there for the wrong reason. She was there for her son. She was sincere. She only wanted to be heard and if Deacon Taylor had not opened his door, she would have gone her own way.

He was rolled into the den. The strange woman stood at the door. She jumped right to the point before Deacon Taylor could ask any questions or remove her from his home. "Dr. Taylor I apologize for disturbing you and your home but I had to come and see you. You

don't know me. My name's Mary Ann. I knew your son Abraham."
The assistant, Deacon Taylor and the strange woman all briefly glanced
into the eyes of each other. Deacon Taylor did not know what the
strange woman was trying to pull but he was not buying her story. She
was not sure if they were on the same page. She continued as Deacon
Taylor and his assistant tried their best to make sense of what she was
saying, "...Well when we were young..."

Mary Ann commenced telling her life story, "My mother took
me south. She'd passed a few years ago but my child and I are here in
New York, now." She did not know what else to say, as she stood at
the door not knowing if she was welcome or barging in on a decent
family.

"Please have a seat," Deacon Taylor insisted. She sat down as
she tightly closed her jacket with her hands in a house that seemed to
be already excruciatingly hot. The assistant passed the strange woman
a glass of water; with one gulp she had finished and passed the glass
back to the assistant empty. "What is your name, young lady?"
Deacon Taylor asked. His mind was racing at the time she was
introducing herself, causing him to have missed her name. Softly she
responded as if she was being questioned by the FBI, "Mary Ann.
Mary Ann Jones." She tried helping Deacon Taylor remember who
she was but her name did not ring any bells. "My mother's name was
Mattie Jones. She was a member of U.C.G.S. Church, some years ago.
I was baptized there. I have no sisters or brothers. My mother was an
Evangelist in the church; and she always fought Pastor Money to allow
more women such as her to preach the word. She was a fighter... I
got pregnant. She was so ashamed... I was only seventeen. She
packed us up and we moved south, where I had my son." Mary Ann
began to weep yet at the same time laugh.

"When my child was born, my mother made me lie. My child
was her child and I was his sister. I was never to tell anyone the truth,
not even my son. Do you know how hard it is, living in a lie for all
those years? I told him on the day we buried my mother. Until this
day, we have not talked about it since."

For a moment the room was silent. Mary Ann got up from her
seat as she spotted an award of Abraham's. She picked it up from the
piano and read it. Deacon Taylor and his assistant looked at one
another then over at Mary Ann. "My son received that for a poem he
read to the young people in the church on youth day, some years ago.
The picture of all the youth is hanging up on the wall." Deacon Taylor
pointed in the direction of a picture, as Mary Ann walked from the

piano to the opposite side of the room where every wall in the room pictures were plastered from top to bottom. She looked intently as she saw not only the picture but also herself at a younger age, standing in the portrait.

She began to quote a poem written by Langston Hughes poem,

Mother to Son:
Well son, I'll tell you:
Life for me ain't been no crystal stair.
It's had tacks in it,
And splinters,
And boards torn up,
And places with no carpet on the floor –
Bare.
But all the time
I'se been a-climbin' on,
And reachin' landin's,
And turnin' corners,
And sometimes goin' in the dark
Where there ain't been no light.
So boy, don't you turn back.
Don't you set down on the steps
'Cause you finds it's kinder hard.
Don't you fall now –
For I'se still goin', honey,
I'se still climbin,'
And life for me ain't been no crystal stair.

Deacon Taylor laughed so hard with joyfulness, "That was the poem Abraham quoted and if I remember, you had helped him memorize it from beginning to end." Mary Ann began to chuckle as she recalled how much it took to remember that poem in one day and recite it in front of the entire church without slipping up on any part. "So, how is Abraham doing these days?" She quickly asked.

Kindly answering but leaving it to Mary Ann's imagination, "he's Abraham." Mary Ann politely requested another glass of water but Deacon Taylor's assistant was not sure if he would miss a part of this story. He quickly went into the kitchen and reappeared back into the den. "Mary Ann are you sure Abraham is the father of your child?" Deacon Taylor did not hesitate to go straight into what they all were trying to get at. "I'm very sure," She replied. "Abraham never knew. I've wanted to say something but I waited so long and after a while I wasn't sure how to say it. My son wanted to know and he is at an age where he should know, who his Daddy is. I mean, he should have known but he's now curious. He's not a problem. I've handled him on my own. My son has more God then I've ever had. He's an 'A' student and on top of his class, at Bishop Edgar A. Love H.S." A smile dashed across her face just when she thought of her son. Mary Ann went on to say as she whispered the most top secret information, "He's accepted the calling on his life. You know... He was called to preach. I guess he's learned from my mother because I haven't been to church in years." She stopped. "Would you like to meet him?" She solicited.

Deacon Taylor gave the impression of being extremely intrigued. The young man was waved in from the car by his mother and in seconds emerged. As he stood there not knowing who was who, they glued their eyes onto him. It was clear as day. His eyes, nose, mouth, hair, skin completion, his height, was all too familiar. Deacon Taylor insisted on raising himself from his wheel chair. His assistant and Mary Ann pitched in to help. He slowly walked over to the young man who stood in his house. "Could it be possible?" Deacon Taylor asked himself. There was no reason for a DNA test because the family genes were all in the boy's face. There was no way he could have been denied, not if they tried.

"Son, what's your name?" The young teenager looked over at his mother, before answering the question. "Emmanuel Taylor Jones." Deacon Taylor stood not much taller then his grandson. They both continued to study one another. "Do you have any idea, who I am?" Deacon Taylor asked looking into his grandsons' eyes, which seemingly looked like those of his own. Emmanuel was very hesitant but ninety percent sure of the answer, "my grandfather, Dr. Richard Taylor.

The doorbell rang. Everyone in the room glanced at each other as Deacon Taylor could only speculate who else it could have been on a day full of questions and surprises. The assistant opened the door and Abraham walked through.

Part Twenty-Two

Aaron and his mother walked together down the street to José's house, with a dish in her hand. They could see from their home a large number of people congregating in front of José's house. "Do you have to work Easter Sunday?" Trustee Jordan asked her son, knowing it was one of the busiest days in the restaurant business. "I'm pretty sure I have to work. I tried calling Lucious and he hasn't been picking up his phone. He never answers the phone on Monday's because he considers it his day. But it's Tuesday and the store is closed. I went up there early today and customers were standing outside wondering what was going on. It's not like Lucious."

Normally, Lucious would schedule his staff who were students during their Easter break as the restaurant is inundated with guests and catering orders. They were one house away, "I'm pretty sure, everything is okay," She confirmed. But in her effort to reassure her son, she wondered if Sarah was having any problem in her pregnancy? Her pregnancy would have caused Lucious not to open his restaurant.

José's entire family must have been standing in front of the house, while his mother and siblings and extended family and friends were in the house. José's mother, Maria, greeted trustee Jordan and Aaron as everyone in the living room looked at them impolitely. "What do we have here?" Maria asked Trustee Jordan as a pot of food is placed in her hands. "This is a soul food dish, called collard greens, it goes well with the pupusas and those fried plantains you made me last time." The family of Maria cordially accepted their new African-American friend.

"Gracias. Mucho gusto." One family member practically slurred out. The mood was cheerful and festive. Maria invited them in as she screamed to other family members in Spanish. Aaron walked over to Juan, José's younger brother who playfully jumped on his back. José's older sister Teresa was busy cleaning up and refilling drinks for all their guests.

Aaron could not get an "A" in Spanish but he was working his way to a C average. "Aaron." The person from the door said as they are looking into the kitchen from backyard. **Reggaetón** music was blaring from the garage. Aaron turned and laughed as José walked toward him with his arm trapped in a cast and tied around his neck in a sling for support. "Qué pasa? Como te va?" José asked Aaron awaiting a response. Teresa jumped in, to help Aaron with his Spanish. "What's happening and how's it going?" They all laughed together.

José began to laugh louder as he described Aaron's reaction to his family in a loud and heavy Spanish accent. "You would've thought he got banged up. He was crying and screaming." Aaron tried to deny José's side of story. "I was just worried for mi amigo."

José pulled out a newspaper. "I'm famous." He turned to page twelve in the local newspaper and showed an article on gang violence in Long Island. "They say I'm the leader of my gang and we are out of control. They even have a picture of me when I was arrested months, ago." Juan started to laugh at José's mug shot placed in the paper. José's mother, Maria ignored the paper but quickly began to talk about another article in the newspaper.

In Maria's deep Salvadoran accent she asked, "Did you know the young couple that was coming from church and wound up in an accident? The poor woman was pregnant. They say she didn't make it and they had to pull the child from her. The baby is in critical condition and the baby might not make it. A Dios mios!" When Aaron closed the paper, he saw a portrait of Lucious and a smaller picture of his truck treacherously flipped upside down on the front page. "What is this?"

Juan directed Aaron in the back room where a gang of young Spanish congregated. As Juan stepped in the room, people looked into everyone's faces and hesitantly followed Juan into the room. Aaron studied the young men. He and José were gang rivals but today, they considered each other a friend. They might consider themselves as friends but everyone was not as willing to accept. Aaron questioned if he had made the right decision but José had not proved him wrong. As of now, Aaron listened to his heart and befriended José.

Aaron felt quite uncomfortable in the room. He did not feel welcomed and without guessing or wasting another second, he asked his business for being there. "Why am I here?" Juan answered with hatred as his friends continued to listen, "Amigo, we have to pay them back for what they've done to my hermano." Juan stood eye-to-eye, toe-to-toe with Aaron. Juan continued to say with conviction, "We fight. You in or out? Amigo?" Juan demanded.

Aaron looked Juan ferociously in his eyes as they stood inches away from each other. José opened the door to the room with his good hand. Aaron was silent but deeply questioned the friendship he has made with José. Aaron was fearful for not only his life but for José's life as well as Juan who cared less if he should live or die. Aaron voice was so loud, he roared, "You wanna die? You wanna go out there and kill'em? You down with this?" He dove into José face, while pointing at Juan and his gang members disguised as friends.

Maria barged into the room. Trustee Jordan was on her heels as they both jostled their way into the bedroom. "José. Juan. What's the problem?" Maria asked as she looked around the room at the face of killers. "Aaron. Why were you yelling?" Trustee Jordan asked her son as she too looked around the room of disheartening young men. No one answered but Trustee Jordan could tell her son was not himself. She politely tried giving Aaron a way out. "Maria thanks for your hospitality but we have to go." But Aaron did not budge. He waited for José's answer to his questions.

Aaron placed everyone in the room, including Juan, on the spot. "I left gang bangin' and I'm not tryin' to get myself killed for no one. If that's what you want then I guess you and your amigos can get killed on your own." Maria and Trustee Jordan stood in front of their sons' faces so they could unmistakably and unequivocally know the truth. Whether their sons were still in gangs and ready to go out and kill over José's battle.

"No." José quickly yelled out and defended himself. "No Ma." Aaron said peacefully as he looked at José still waiting for his response.

José stepped in the center of the crowd. Some of the young Spanish gang members shifted their bodies as they criminally waited to commit a crime. They look around at one another trying to figure out who would make the first move and prove the wrong point. José tried to say a few words to keep the peace but by him leaving the gang, his words held no power. As an outsider he had to watch his back from not only rivalry gang members but also the gang he had left. He was alone and hopeless until Aaron had mailed him a Christmas card. Aaron may never know he saved José's life by mailing a one-dollar Christmas card to José while he was in jail. He had placed twenty dollars in it but saving his life was priceless. *If God saved me the least I can do is try to help my brother and my friends.* "I do not want this. We can't keep killing each other. We've lost too many and I say, enough. I will not have blood on my hands. If you are with me, then you will end this, today.

A second felt like eternity as everyone took in what José had finish saying. He never planned this and had no clue about what was taking place in his house. He would have to consider what was just said by Aaron and what took place with the boys he once saw as family. The adolescent gang members grilled José and Aaron down. They stormed out of the room and out the house. The hallway was packed with curious family members. The few that remained could only wonder what was next. Juan pushed himself past his family and followed the other gang members out the door. Maria tried to impede but José took hold of his crying mother with an assuring look. She kept from chasing after her youngest child and darted past the crowded room and into her bedroom.

"Ma, we gotta leave," Aaron declared as he handed the newspaper with the front page visible to his mother for her to see. She had a dilemma as she looked up at him. She did not want to believe the images from the article. "Lucious is in trouble," He barked not caring about those who surrounded them. Trustee Jordan took her son by the hand and together they walked out of the house.

Part Twenty-Three

The job of the Chairman of the Deacon Board was never done. The phone kept ringing and ringing. Deacon Taylor read every local newspaper and watched Rebecca Stanton report Sarah's death over the nightly news. In his condition, all Deacon Taylor felt he could do was pray for Lucious' strength. As the tragic accident broadcast over the local news channel, Deacon Taylor sat in prayer. Unsure, whether he should go to the hospital but he followed the direction of the Pastor. He was instructed not to flood Lucious with calls and visits. Deacon Taylor followed his Pastors' instructions. Pastor Money would visit on behalf of the church and would distinguish what the family needed.

Deacon Taylor closed his eyes and began to talk to God, aloud. "Oh Lord. I have been there. I know what it felt like to loss a person closest to humanly love. I cried and you heard my cry. I thought I could not live another day but you've allowed me to see all these years. I've lived. I hurt today because I knew my time with my wife would surely come to end and I cherished the moments you have given me, with her. But this young man needs you. He too will be able to go on, with you at his side. We do not understand but we know there is a reason. May he be given strength and may he know you are there. You have never forsaken him and during his time of hurt, may he understand it more then ever. Protect his child; give the child a chance to walk the earth. Remove his pain and what suffering he endures. May he learn from it and may it be as short as the time we truly live on this earth. This is my prayer to you Father. Amen."

Just then the phone rang and promptly God answered Deacon Taylor's' prayer. "Hello? Hello? Is there someone there? Please speak up, if there is someone there." Deacon Taylor called out. He thought there was no one but a desperate voice tenderly spoke with enormous amount of pain. "It's me, Deacon Taylor, Lucious." A smile of thanks brushed Deacon Taylor's aged face but tried to conceal his hurt in the tone of his voice for Lucious. Deacon Taylor allowed Lucious to lead in the conversation, without saying a word. He understood that the call was meant for him to be a listener and the person who he had come to know was hurting.

Deacon Taylor could hear Lucious' hurt as he exposed his pain on Deacon Taylor's heart. "She was supposed to be here with me." He began to cry out. "We were to grow old and have lots of children.

What happened? WHY?" He cried to Deacon Taylor. "My daughter is fighting for her life. But how will I raise a child a girl without her mother? I was depending on Sarah to nurture our children, we had a deal. I do not know what to do." Deacon Taylor was quietly listening; Lucious had to make sure he was still there paying attention. "Deacon Taylor, can I ask you a question?" Deacon Taylor responded to his agonizing friend. "You can, my friend. Ask." He insisted. "Am I wrong for not praying to God for my first child's life? In some ways I'm afraid. I'm afraid if she lives, I will not know what to do and if she doesn't make it..." Lucious hesitated but continued. "It was meant for me not to have her. All those tubes and machines connected to her tiny body. Will she even have a chance to make it out of all this, and for what; not to have known who her mother was? I was not the best husband. I hardly am the best Christian. So, how well will I do as a single father to a girl?" Deacon Taylor waited until Lucious let it all out, including his tears and expressions of grief before beginning to minister to the broken hearted man.

"My son, God loves you. He knows your pain and He knows quite well what you can and can not bare. You need to have faith because He will be the only one who will set you free from this hurt. I've prayed for your daughter and God has already answered my prayer. Sometimes, when you do not want to talk to God, he will talk to you through someone, someway, somehow.

Deacon Taylor clearly understood Lucious' suffering. He continued to minister to Lucious. After a long pause and silence in their phone conversation, they tried controlling their raging emotions. "Lucious, I have buried my wife, my son, my grandchildren, sisters, brothers, parents and friends. You know what? I shall meet with them one day. God had work for me to do and that is why He has kept me so long. I did not know why He kept me but he did and I've cried many times by myself to God. But you know what, Lucious? He kept me here long enough to tell a broken heart, like you, tomorrow the sun will shine and a new day will come forth for you to look back and thank Him for bringing you out of it all. You will see it as I have. It will be your revelation, a miracle that you will share will others. He will give you strength as He did for me. You just need to believe. Hallelujah!" Deacon Taylor began to speak in tongues.

"Lucious is there anything I can do for you and your family in this time of need?" Deacon Taylor asked. Lucious thought about it and remembered the young people in the church and the Rap Session came to mind. "Who will handle the kids' Rap Session at the church?

They will be so disappointed and I wish I could be there for them..."
Lucious murmured.

Deacon Taylor had not been able to go as frequently due to his health. He believed in the vision of the young people's Rap Session and wanted to see its success, so he quickly volunteered. He hid the fact that it was a long process in finding the right, young, dedicated Christian for the class. They had three thousand members, one-fourth of them were men. One-fourth of the men were active young members of the church. One percent of those young, active men were willing to take on a responsibility. Deacon Taylor knew Lucious was called for a reason. He knew if the church had to find another Lucious, the assignment would lose its purpose. God never took back an assignment unfinished. "I will talk to our Pastor but I'll accept the task of running the youth ministry at the church. I'm like Michael Jordan, coming out of retirement, except they'll have to roll me up and down the court." Lucious chuckled for a moment with Deacon Taylor.

"Is there a topic and scripture you wish for me to discuss?" Deacon Taylor asked. Lucious could not think straight and all the material he had to instruct the class was left at his home.

Lucious was in the hospital for the past two days. "I don't know, Deacon Taylor. Oh! But you can call Aaron Jordan, Trustee Jordan's son and Emmanuel Jones. They both work in my restaurant and are great at helping in the class.

Deacon Taylor inaudibly spoke to himself. Lucious wondered if Deacon Taylor was paying attention or having trouble hearing what he was saying over the phone. "Is Emmanuel Jones a member of U2 Can Get Saved?" Deacon Taylor asked as he stumbled over words. Lucious didn't think anything of the question asked by his mentor but briefed him on Emmanuel.

That evening Deacon Taylor invited Abraham, Emmanuel and Mary Ann back over to his home. His assistant gladly prepared dinner and set the table for what could be a memorable day for all of their lives to come. Mary Ann and Abraham drove up in separate cars to Deacon Taylor's home on a breezy, rainy evening. They sat in their cars as they waited for one another to go into the house, first. In an uncomfortable situation Emmanuel hopped out of his mothers' passenger side of the car and headed toward the house. He never thought he would have met his father let alone his grandfather.

He was not about to let his parents' childish emotions get in his way. Emmanuel rung the door bell and waited for someone to answer. His father and mother walked up behind him. The assistant opened the door and grinned, as the guests walked in from out of the rain. He thought as he retrieved their raincoats and hats, *this is going to be like one of those reality TV shows, these young people enjoy so much.* As if he was one of the invited guests, the assistant sat in his usual seat, forgetting for a second he was preparing the dinner.

Abraham shot into his father's bedroom (chambers); guilty as charged but pleaded his case before his father met the others in the den (courtroom). "I know the kid is mine but come on..." Abraham attempted to whisper. "She goes away for years and pops back up with a kid? Why did she wait until now to say something?" All the while, Deacon Taylor is listening but not listening to his sons' rhetoric. Deacon Taylor spoke in a loud roar, not caring to be discrete. "The child is yours. This is not about you. This is about a child who has been given a chance to see his family for the first time..." Deacon Taylor silenced himself, controlling his temper and thoughts, when he really wanted to jump out of his wheel chair and lash at his son. "I told you before. A true man judges himself and his success not by how much money he has in the bank or how many houses he owns but by his children's success in life. After providing and giving all you can give to help your child grow to live a prosperous life, the worst thing a father could face is his child living an unproductive life or worst burying them. But thank God, He judges based on a man's heart."

Abraham was lost for words. He understood his fate. He accepted his sentence, reluctantly. He would do what was best. Although, he would listen to his father's wisdom, he for sure was far from pleased with the verdict. Deacon Taylor stopped his son before leaving the bedroom. Deacon Taylor, who is the Judge in the courtroom, has made his decision and a severe punishment was given. "Son, listen to your father. Your son needs his father; like you needed me in your time of need. I was not there for you. I was angry. I worked so hard to leave all the bad things behind... I was dealing with one son on drugs and in prison and your older brother, well... I let you both down because I could not face my own anger. I was never able to tell your older brother sorry before he left this earth. It was not for me to judge his life. He was wrong then and I still believe it's wrong, now. But he was my son.

Truth Of The Matter

I could not talk to you, when you needed me to listen. I was wrong and I'm sorry. I worked so hard to give you and your brother a good life; more than I ever had and I was disappointed. I could have died then. Who would I leave my legacy and fortune with when your mother and I left the earth? My choices were an alcoholic son or a son with AIDS on his death bed. My life was sucked out of me and I had nothing to live for." Deacon Taylor paused for a second. "But I will not let you tell that boy in there, it was not your fault or anything else. He deserves a father."

"It's not like you have to pay child support. The boy is about to graduate." Abraham looked his father square in his eyes. He laughed as he thought about it. They continued onto the dining room, with the last thought of the day by Deacon Taylor for Abraham.

Mary Ann and Emmanuel sat in the den as they awaited Deacon Taylor to roll in from his bedroom. Abraham, still apprehensively followed his father in the den, where the woman he once laid with, the woman who birthed his child, sat in his presence after seventeen years. You could hear a pin drop as everyone waited until Deacon Taylor set the tone of the dinner meeting. Deacon Taylor rolled around the den as he showed Emmanuel the picture of his new found family. Mary Ann and Abraham silently glanced at one another as they watched their son get schooled by his grandfather. He had so much catching up to do but Emmanuel tried absorbing every bit of information he received from Deacon Taylor. The assistant walked into the den to announce, "Dinner is ready to be served. Please follow me to the dining room."

The elegant setting of the table astonished all of Deacon Taylor's guests. It was his best Chinaware. His guests felt as if they were invited to eat at the King's table for dinner. Abraham knew the history behind the chinaware but Emmanuel had a lot to learn about the history of his family. He saw pictures but nothing was more moving to Emmanuel until Deacon Taylor explained the past and their accentors chinaware sets.

"My mother use to clean this old Jewish woman's house. She worked for her for over twenty years. That old Jewish woman counted every piece of silverware and chinaware for some years. She thought my mother did not know but she did. She didn't trust my mother as far as she could see her. But when my mother remarried..." Before Deacon Taylor could go any further, Mary Ann shouted across the table as if she was being given a quiz and brightly knew the answer. "She gave your mother this stuff for her wedding present." The assistant walked back into the kitchen shaking his head. Deacon Taylor disregarded her impromptu response and Abraham laughed to himself. "No, that old Jewish woman never gave my mother anything but a pay check. But one day she realized my mama was her only friend.

Needless to say, when she died and had her 'home going service,' my mama was the only person who signed the guest book." Everyone sat quietly at the table until Deacon Taylor laughed so loud they thought he was going to have a convulsion. Mary Ann quickly asked in her squeaky voice, "So she gave your mother all of this chinaware, right?" The table all looked at one other as Deacon Taylor responded. "Yes, she gave my mother all of this stuff and the rest of her inheritance went to the state. My mama was so surprised to have gotten this." Emmanuel looked at his grandfather as he sat diagonally across from him. "Sir, that's a great lesson on being grateful." Deacon Taylor momentary took a glimpse at Emmanuel from the tip of his glasses, wondering how Mary Ann and her mother raised such a bright child. "I told yah, my baby is somethin' smart," Mary Ann shouted across the table as she was smiling from ear to ear. "Yes, your son is very bright." He said to Mary Ann. "That is a great story on being grateful," Deacon Taylor said to Emmanuel with a smile. "Let us pray and bless the food."

Deacon Taylor prayed over the food and gave a special prayer to Lucious and his family, for his new family and for Emmanuel's welcoming home celebration. "Pop, how is the kid doing? I read the paper; that's horrible. He and his wife seemed like good people." Abraham said, leaving it at that. "What happened?" Mary Ann asked. Emmanuel tried explaining the situation while everyone's eyes were glued to his mouth as he described his boss.

"Lucious cared about us. He keeps on top of Aaron at work but for good reasons. Plus, Shemaiah, this girl who goes to my school and attends U2 Can Get Saved Church stayed after school everyday just to talk with his wife. I don't know, without him keeping everybody out of trouble by giving them jobs and talking to us during Rap Session kids are going to go back to doing all the wrong things. We are told to become our own leaders but that's easier said then done. People get killed for lesser things than trying to be a leader." Emmanuel said, as he looked Deacon Taylor in his eyes.

"Lucious and his wife, at least reminded me of the people back home. In the South, people cared and talked to one another. Mrs. Bell always smiled and said nice things to us. They call where I am from the 'Bible Belt' because everything stopped on Sunday's for worship. Lucious and Mrs. Bell made me think about the south and oh how I miss it. I pray for his recovery. I pray for his strength and I pray for his child.

Deacon Taylor asked Emmanuel a few questions about where they went to church, school, friends and his future. As they went deep into their conversation, Mary Ann and Abraham dug into their food. They did not look up but to drink from their glasses and back down for more. Deacon Taylor said, "Lucious did tell me you attend our Rap Session with the young people at the church." They were glad to have something in common, church. They talked the entire dinner about the Bible as his parents went straight for dessert.

"Abraham," Deacon Taylor called. "Explain from the beginning how you and Mary Ann met and how everything came about. I think my grandchild deserves an explanation. He's been lied to enough in one lifetime, now let him hear the truth." Emmanuel grinned as his grandfather winked at him. Abraham looked over at Mary Ann. Mary Ann looked over at Deacon Taylor. Deacon Taylor looked over at his assistant. "What?" The assistant asked as the dinner table got quiet and stared in his direction. "What are you doin'?" Mary Ann asked. The assistant placed the video camera on the counter and sinfully glared at the family. "I'm making a documentary," He said as he tried to resume. "About what?" Deacon Taylor asked. "About today's dysfunctional families."

The old assistant could not keep a straight face when he answered his friend. "I'm thinking about calling it... Bad Families Gone Worst." It took a split second for the family to realize he was serious. "Turn that thing off and get out of here. You keep watching those reality TV shows. I told you that stuff is ruining people." Deacon Taylor hollered as his assistant miserably walked away.

Abraham began to falter in his words before he could finish the first sentence. He looked Emmanuel in the eye as he spoke. "We were about your age or a little younger, when your mother got pregnant. She didn't tell me and now here you are. If I..." Mary Ann cut him off before he could go any further in laying blame on her. "I admit, I didn't directly tell you but I said something to you and you'd played dumb. We went to town hall to get married and everything." Deacon Taylor was stunned by what Mary Ann had just said. "Who got married? How did you?" Deacon Taylor asked both parents. Abraham knew she had just set off a world of questions, leaving no other choice but to come clean. "We were married in town hall; we forged the papers and lied about our age. The witnesses were some strange couple standing by waiting to get married themselves. The next thing I know, she moved. We were in love and head over heels for one another," Abraham said to his son.

Deacon Taylor marveled over the situation. It was one thing to not have known about his grandson's existence but to find out his son was married to this woman. What else was there? Abraham quickly answered the obvious question running in his father's mind, before he was asked the question. "I was not married to her." He was speaking about the wife his father thought he eloped with and had children with.

Part Twenty-Four

The Mayor, local politicians and other preachers stood together with Pastor Money at a press conference to rid the town of all gangs. They were looking for alternatives for after-school programs, jobs and other activities. The town would rid the streets of what they saw was a serious gang problem. The local television station and newspaper representatives stood tightly around the stoop of U.C.G.S. Church. The Mayor in his gentle tone of voice, off-the-clearance-rack dark suit, dreary tie, unadventurous light blue dress shirt and conservative over worn shoes; was no match for Pastor Money and the other clergy. Their suits were tailored to their likings.

Their shoes either were snake or ostrich skin with a bold statement. Unlike the Mayor, they climbed out of the best foreign cars and captured the attention of their parishioners who came out in support of their Pastors. Their voices demanded attention but the Clergymen waited patiently for their turn to speak into the microphone. Their voices moved the emotion of the crowd. The leaders of the town tried their best to show support for the cause but lines were drawn between the community leaders on politic and church. Another line was clearly being drawn between the youth on the streets.

Pastor Money stood at the podium as his fellow clergymen, congregation, community, media broadcast and elderly all supported his message. On a cloudy day in May, in front of less than a hundred people and in preparation for rain to come, Pastor Money spoke to the crowd as though he was Dr. Martin Luther King Jr. speaking on Washington in front of thousands of people.

"If all these supposedly-for- the- Black People organizations are getting so much federal funding for the kids, then what seems to be the problem? We have more churches in our community than any other neighborhood, so why are our children in the worst condition than they were the day we migrated from the South to the North in large numbers with no education, no money and nowhere to go? Our young folks have an opportunity to get an education but they are not taking full advantage it. They do not have faith and are too impatient. Let's not make any excuses for our young people but do not make excuses for why we are not preparing them, either.

They are more than welcome in the house of the Lord. We have a program for our young people. It is called, The Rap Session.

These young people can come and discuss matters they deal with on a regular basis and I tell you; I've learned from my young people by just sitting in one of their classes. And we feed them.

All these Black organizations, youth centers, social development agencies in our community should come from the basis of the church. Now, really. Let's be honest. Where are these organizations and what are they really doing for our young ones? The **Truth of the Matter** is: there are more offices federally funded in our communities to help rid these problems but look around, they bring extra problems. They place all the shelters, half-way-houses, sex offenders and rehab centers next to your homes and build businesses on the other side of town.

Town Hall, not-for-profit organizations, police departments, shopping centers, not even our schools should **NOT** be the focal point of our neighborhoods but the church. The community is too busy fighting the preachers. The churches are too busy worrying about membership but let's start worrying about the future of our young people. If you do not give much then do not expect much. But the Bible says, for much is given, much is expected.

W.E.B Dubois and Booker T. Washington were two of the most well known scholars of our time and they debated publicly in reference to what they thought was best for the African-American people. W.E.B. Dubois felt Blacks should concentrate on education; while Booker T. Washington believed Black people should have a skill. What would they debate today? Our young people are not being educated and hardly any of them are going to trade schools for a skill. What we have learned in the past is obsolete and these children are training and teaching themselves. That is dangerous." Pastor Money began to "wooo!" the crowd. But if Jesus were here, there would be no debates and choices and no press conference. The decision would be made on his return."

The crowd stood still as the rain lightly drizzled on their wrinkled faces. Pastor Money was impressed by the message he delivered; it could not have been better said. If he had given his sermon for another occasion, he would have taken an offering for such a moving speech.

The young people from the near by Bishop Edgar A. Love High School enrolled with young Black and Hispanic teenagers were released from school a half hour before the press conference begun. The town police followed a normal routine as mobs of inquisitive African-American teenagers walked hastily to their homes from school.

Truth Of The Matter

Some of the rowdy teenagers looked for a little mischief; the others looked straight with a mission to get into their houses safe and sound. In large numbers, they walked passed abandoned and boarded up homes and businesses which surrounded U.C.G.S' newly constructed mega church. The youth began to march through the crowd made of elders as the organizers against gang violence started to disburse from the church.

Their school administration walked with walkie-talkies as they tried to alleviate any small act of childhood behaviors. The last thing the Mayor of the village, Pastor Money and the community leaders wanted were a clash between the young and old people of the community. Everyone quickly seemed to have gone to "code red" as they tried to rush the young crowd forward.

Emmanuel and a small group of Hempstead teenagers marched their way to the podium. Pastor Money and other clergymen started moving the old parishioners swiftly to their cars but they all froze in position. Emmanuel gestured for one of the local officials to hand him the microphone but after a few seconds, Emmanuel forced his way in front of the podium and snatched the microphone. His young followers including Isaiah, José and Aaron who had planned to come from his private school to be at Emmanuel's side as he arranged to address the community. Emmanuel looked over the crowd filled with his peers and older community leaders. His voice began to crack, showing his nervousness. But after the first few words, Emmanuel spoke fervently to his followers and leaders.

"We are God's children. We are not animals. We are the future." Rebecca Stanton, the news reporter, directed the camera man to follow along. "They call us worthless, killers, murderers, the devil's children. But we are God's children. And there comes a time when every generation must stand up. Each young generation holds back their greatest fear and become fighters for the legacy of hope. Where is our hope? Do we not hope for greatness? Do we not wish to become great leaders, one day? But how can our generation become leaders if our entire hope is gone?

Emmanuel continued to say as his school administration, Pastor, grandfather and his fellow listeners took in every word uttered from his mouth. "The world is watching us kill one another. Our own leaders have thrown in the towel. Our friends are dying before our own eyes and frankly I can't watch television because of the violence." Emmanuel paused as he looked over at Deacon Taylor. The rain began to fall but no one budged. "Years ago four young men like ourselves standing before you took a bold stand." Emmanuel glanced over at José, Aaron and Isaiah. They decided enough was enough. "Those four Black college students sat at a counter in Greensboro, North Carolina. At that time it was very racist and segregated. You could not sit at the counter or in the restaurant if you were a Colored man. They walked into that restaurant in Greensboro, North Carolina and sat peacefully at that counter. Those four college students who took part in that sit-in were no older than us. They had hope. They had hoped that one day, you and I would not have to go into the very same restaurant from the back door. They had hope. They hoped we would never be denied the privilege of living in a free society. They had hope. They hoped you and I would use them as an example to stand up for ourselves. They had hope. They hoped that they would leave a legacy that would change the world and make it a better place."

Rebecca Stanton at this point had shoved her way to the front of the audience. Umbrellas hovered over people's heads. Some of the most elderly stood in the door of the church, protected from the rain, while others cracked open the windows of their cars to hear Emmanuel's speech. This was the path to all the students who lived on the Park Side area of Hempstead. But the path was blocked off and the student congregated at the front of the church. The petrified elders became at ease. The police department was not on alert but had put down their guard. The elected officials were gleaming.

"Who is willing to stand up with the four of us and make a difference? Who is willing to fight but for a different reason? We are not afraid to fight but are we willing to stop fighting each other? If you are willing to help us, tomorrow at school, we will need you all to sign our petition. I need us to sign it and commit to fighting differently. I'm not telling you not to fight but to fight for our own lives. Who's with me? The crowd roared. The students became rambunctious as they paraded in small circles. Emmanuel, Isaiah, José and Aaron smirked at each other.

In minutes, the block was cleared of people and the town employees were stripping the equipment off the steps as everyone rushed out of the rain. The doors of the church were locked. Pastor Money and a few members, including Deacon Taylor were heading to their cars. Deacon Taylor's assistant secured his wheel chair in the vehicle as Deacon Taylor stared out his fogged window he noticed from a short distance a dark skin, medium built, Black man standing outside of a car looking back at him in the rain. "Don't move," Deacon Taylor yelled to his assistant as he shifted his glasses to get a better look at the strange man. The rain heavily on his van and the strange man did not move or escape into his car to get away from the rain.

Deacon Taylor gasped for air as he recognized Lucious standing in the rain. "Lower me down," Deacon Taylor demanded of his assistant. "Excuse me, sir?" His assistant questioned. "Lower my wheel chair down, NOW. It's Lucious." His assistant lowered Deacon Taylor into the pouring rain.

Lucious walked over to Deacon Taylor. Understanding the severity of Lucious' action as he stood in the rain, Deacon Taylor remained silent. "My wife's body will be buried tomorrow." Lucious murmured as the rain masked his tears. "I will have to bury my wife, a week after mother's day," He cried as his voice turned to anger. "She fought for those children. She wanted to make a difference but now she'll be buried next to all the children who saw no hope. While they were busy killing one another on the streets, over gangs, she was putting her life on the line to educate them. Somebody tell me why? I pray my wife did not die in vein!

Her dream was to open a youth center; no one knew it but me. She believed there was hope. I didn't." He said, confused over her death and not his own.

"But…I will be strong. I have to be strong for my daughter. I believe God has a purpose. I don't know what, but I can only imagine. I know what I will have to do and I'm pretty sure Sarah would have been quite please with her old man. Please keep me in prayer," Lucious said as he shook Deacon Taylor's hand and they parted ways.

Proverbs 19:18 "Discipline your son while there is hope, but do not indulge your angry resentments by undue chastisements and set yourself to his ruin."

Proverbs 22:6 "Train up a child in the way he should go: and when he is old, he will not depart from it."

Proverbs 29:7 "Correct your son and he will give you rest; yes, he will give delight to your heart."

Part Twenty-Five

Many students who participated in the Rap Session at U.C.G.S. attended Sarah's funeral. A month later, the class tried to resume and carry on with its usual upbeat spirit. The church had ordered pizza since Lucious' restaurant was closed indefinitely. No one was sure how soon Lucious would get back into the swing of things but his business was well missed. A sign was posted on the door for patrons and employees to read. His cellular phone was disconnected. His home phone was full of messages and his newly purchased Ford Explorer must have been in the garage because it was never seen. Neighbors were not sure and his mother gave very little information.

Deacon Taylor tried to reach him but was forced to only assume he still needed some time to himself. But Pastor Money and Deacon Taylor were thrilled to see the class had tripled since the press conference and the entire buzz about what the young people were getting out of the class. A couple of well respected parishioners, who were liked by the younger people, joined in the class discussion. The class had well over seventy teenagers crammed into one room. Deacon Taylor, Pastor Money and the two other adults wondered if it would be best to split the class in half.

"No." Deacon Taylor insisted. "These young people are here to have a forum and we are going to do as Lucious would have done; and that is hold a forum. We can not change the format of this class but we will need two microphones; one microphone with a stand, in the center of the room allowing order and one speaker at any given time and the other for me. Oh! See if we can use the computers, get them uncovered and unlocked for the young people to work with, I was told they come in handy." Deacon Taylor was informed by Aaron and Emmanuel of how they assisted Lucious by looking up scriptures on his lap top. Pastor Money was skeptical but gave permission for the computers to be used during the class under Deacon Taylor's guidance.

Deacon Taylor and his adult helpers walked back into the church dining room/auditorium, to call the forum to order. Emmanuel, giving a special prayer for Lucious and his family, opened the class with a prayer. The food was blessed and class rules were given, read aloud by Aaron; who was asked by Deacon Taylor to help keep the Rap Session in the church for the young people. Emmanuel was Deacon Taylor's personal assistant in the class, while Aaron referred to the topics, information and the scriptures on-line.

Deacon Taylor was impressed with today's technology; and as much as he did not need help locating any scriptures, he was fearful how quickly the youth retrieved their information from the internet. "Like all things in life, if it used the wrong way it will cause wrong things to happen but if it is used for the right purpose then I guess we will get good things from it. Simple." Deacon Taylor tried to forewarn his students the purpose of the computer. Isaiah chimed in, "like eating in moderation, so you don't end up like..." He said while looking at Shemaiah.

Deacon Taylor, like Lucious felt the use of the computers brought a youthful touch to the table. He hoped the young people, while playfully looking up websites relating to the Bible and strictly on the matter at hand, would not detour into forbidden websites. He welcomed the fact he was being taught by a new generation of thinkers.

"Subject is: **Teaching and Sharing Information vs. Keeping Knowledge to one's self**.

I want three people to be my computer wizards and look up on the website, what the Bible says about being knowledgeable. I want you to tell me what scriptures the computer suggests." Aaron was already on the computer. José sat in a seat next to him and worked off the same computer. Isaiah and Shemaiah jumped on the other two computers.

"Yo! Deacon, I found what you were looking for," Aaron said with enthusiasm but Deacon Taylor just looked over at him for a second. He carefully tilted his glasses down as he indicated his dislike to how he was addressed. Although, Aaron and the other classmates showed signs of honor to Deacon Taylor it was no honor and not respectful to be addressed as, "Yo". Young people were too comfortable for his taste and to him it was disrespectful. Deacon Taylor interrupted the class as some of the students stood around Aaron as they played on the computer. His voice demanded attention and with a microphone it claimed authority.

"Young people I do not think it is appropriate to call an older man who had picked cotton to eat until I moved to New York; fought in world war two in my early twenties; shined shoes to get through college; who was hosed during the Civil Rights movements. My oldest son was attacked by dogs and you fill you can address me as "Yo"! I earned the right to be addressed by "Sir" because I was the first Black to teach at your local high school; first Black principal in this area; a man who stood beside Dr. Martin Luther King Jr. I taught your present principal. Needless to say, I'm an old man in a wheel chair and old enough to be your grandfather. I have lived this earth for close to a century. When you can claim my rap sheet then you can earn, what little respect I demand; until then I think I have earned the right to be addressed as, "Sir". If that is too much then I suggest the next best thing you call me is "Mister". As a matter of fact, I believe anyone old enough to be your parent should be given respect. They should be called "Sir" or "Maám". Do you agree?"

The class looked around the room as Deacon Taylor stared in the eyes of his audience. He could only imagine it would take more time and reassurance for these young people to accept what he had just asked of them. Isaiah, trying to be a wise guy, began to applaud Deacon Taylor causing a slow but thunderous standing ovation from seventy young people who were never more moved then by Deacon Taylor's speech. After, they all settled into their seats, Deacon Taylor, in a softer approach, continued to say, "I want to hear you address people differently. I want you to say yes Ma'am or yes Sir. This is the ultimate sign of respect and it will help you go far. I want you to learn not only to respect your elders but also to humble yourself in front of people who led the path. And I know if we were not in the walls of this church and in your schools, one of you would have rolled this old man down a flight of steps. Just kidding." He and the class laughed as he looked at the faces of those who quietly thought about it instead of laughing about it.

The class agreed silently as the other adults showed signs of agreement by the gargantuan smiles on their faces. Deacon Taylor jumped back into the subject by telling a short story, relating the topic. "As I was being honored at a dinner a few weeks ago, I happened to look around the room. I noticed all the faces were those who were the Black crème of the crème of this neighborhood. Those same people fight to keep one from succeeding past them and prefer you coming to them for information rather than you not needing them at all. You have so-called friends like this: they want to act like they know more than you, have better things than you, and treat you like you are less than them and as if you're the dumb one. Those people do not know or do not want to know; we are all in the same boat trying to get to the same place, HEAVEN. We have to teach one another; only then we can get out of this situation that we call HELL.

Now, let me hear what scriptures you've found on your toys. I'm sorry, computers." Deacon Taylor mentions as he chuckled along with the student body. "The keywords are knowledge, understanding and wisdom."

"Yes SIR." Shemaiah called out loud as the microphone from the center of the room is carried over to her by one of the two adults.

Proverbs 3:13 "Happy is the man who finds wisdom, and the man who gains understanding; for her proceeds are better than the profits of silver, and her gain than fine gold. She is more precious than rubies, and all the things you may desire cannot compare with her. Length of days is in her right hand, in her left hand riches and honor. Her ways are ways of pleasantness, and all her paths are peace. She is a tree of life to those who take hold of her, and happy are all who retain her."

"Thank you. Can one of the men over there sitting beside the young lady in her most creative hair-do give me another?" Deacon Taylor asked, as he and a few others paid close attention to Shemaiah's fashion statement. Yes, SIR," Isaiah screamed out as if he was saluting a Captain in the Armed Services. "I have a scripture found on-line," Isaiah, continued to yell.

Proverbs 16:16 "How much better it is to get wisdom than gold! And to get understanding is to be chosen rather than silver."

"Thank you, young man. Deacon Taylor said. "Anyone else?" Deacon Taylor asked. "Yes SIR." José grabbed the microphone and yelled out trying his hardest to speak through his heavy accent.

Ecclesiastes 7:12 "It says... but the excellence of knowledge is that wisdom gives life to those who have it."

"Thank you. I see a hand in the back of the room." Deacon Taylor said. "Emmanuel come up to the center and read the scripture. Use the microphone, so I can hear you. Emmanuel held the microphone but with the Bible at his side as he began to recite two scriptures.

Proverbs 24:3-4 "Through wisdom a house is built, and by understanding it is established; by knowledge the rooms are filled with all precious and pleasant riches."

Ecclesiastes 7:19 "Wisdom strengthens the wise more than ten rulers of the city."

"Thank you SIR," Emmanuel said. He smiled over at his grandfather, whose glasses tilted down from his eyes, as he cheerfully noticed his grandson's knowledge of the Bible.

Deacon Taylor explained the three major words: knowledge, understanding and wisdom. The students were intrigued by the discussion and before long the forum had ended. There were some heavy and poignant subjects covered in a short period of time on: **teaching and sharing information vs. keeping the knowledge to one's self.** Deacon Taylor learned more today then any of the students. He was thankful to see young people using a tool he himself knew nothing about and how they used today's technology to find out information dealing with the Bible. His aide waited patiently off to the side as the young people surrounded a person who they had a new found respect for as a leader. The questions continued to pour out well after the class had been closed with prayer.

Pastor Money quickly seized the microphone in an attempt to rescue the elderly celebrity. "Did we not enjoy this class?" He asked as the young people deafeningly clapped their hands in unison to show their satisfaction. Now, Deacon Taylor and I are some old men and we need our rest, after we hear from our political leaders that have paid us a visit out of their busy schedule. If you are still here, I will have no other choice but to pass the collection plate around." Laughter burst out from the audience but they did not notice Pastor Money's seriousness. The crowded room faced the politicians who came to spread their message on gang violence.

Although, the young people had heard the same message throughout their school and newspapers had been printing stories on the violence relating to gangs; the subject seemed to have fallen to the waist side. Some of the young people held their own conversations, while others began to sneak out of the back of the church. Before the last politician had finished speaking, the over seventy people who they began with quickly turned into a dismal half. The students, who decided to remain, stayed reluctantly. Deacon Taylor, Pastor Money and the politicians could only shake their heads knowing that they had reached their limits; and prayer at this point was all they could do. The children did not want to hear what they were saying about gangs because those were their friends.

It was already a quarter past ten on a humid late spring, Friday night. Aaron, Jose and many others were able to sneak out of Rap Session. They debated on their destination at the corner of the church. "I can go get my Mom's car and we can head out or hang out at your house," Aaron said to José. They walked south toward their block on South Franklin with their Bibles in their hands. "Yo! Can you believe we are graduating in a couple of weeks?" Aaron said to José, who was showing signs of pain. José struggled as his good arm turned tired from the toting of his Bible but he pressed on and persevered. There was no need for Aaron's assistance. "Are you alright?" Aaron asked firmly. José without another word took refuge at the corner bodega; a block away from their homes.

Aaron remained outside talking to a few of his old gang members. There was no resentment toward him since his friends saw him always as the church boy. The **Truth of the Matter** was: some of his old gang members had less respect for him when he had first joined the gang. They wondered why he got down in the first place. He was always challenged but was head strong and unpredictable. They knew he would always choose to do right when they were headed in the wrong direction, yet he was still tested on his loyalty. When he wanted out, they saw the same Aaron but a stronger person. He told them straight up, "God has something better for me. I no longer want to be a part of this but something greater than all of us. I'm loyal to God," He told them with his head held down, waiting for the worst and praying for his life.

His old gang members were dressed in normal over sized True Religion jeans, S-Carter sneakers, enormous sized white-T shirts, fitted baseball caps, half carrying cell phones while the other half carried I-pods and danced about as they walked up to Aaron. With no obvious gang paraphernalia except for small red accents in their clothing, they looked Aaron up and down while he stood in front of the Bodega with a Bible in his hand. It was almost as if the day repeated itself, when he removed his membership from their rooster; choosing Gospel over Gangster.

Aaron looked over at José as he walked out of the Bodega pulling candy, chips and other surprises from his pockets; all the while tightly gripping his Bible in his arm sling which held his arm in position from his gun shot wounds. As he stood beside Aaron looking into the eyes of his enemies, Aaron tapped him without alarming his old gang members. José gave the impression of being unafraid and not moved by Aaron's people and his old rival from when he was once in his gang. He was not going to play it down because they were still enemies. Aaron tapped José, a second time; this time making it obvious to the young men who were eyeing José down. José looked Aaron unswervingly in his eyes to make sure he and everyone else knew he was not afraid of any of them. "No. Look," Aaron whispered, causing the rest of the gang members to turn and stare simultaneously in the opposite direction, Aaron and José were looking. José's old gang members were a block away; marching swiftly toward Aaron's old gang. José's younger brother, Juan was leading the Salvadorian gang adorned with paraphernalia colors double the size of Aaron's friends. José hastily met his brother and his posse half way, a yard away from Aaron as his gang. "What's going on Juan?" José asked and the crowd demonically looked past him and in the direction of their opposition. Juan, the symbol of a chief going into war and preparing other warriors, began to speak boastfully, while his hands mimicked the rhythm of his speech. "These hombre muertos tried to kill you and we gonna kill'dem." Both sides started yelling in the direction of the other. No one showed any weapons but José and Aaron knew if they did not talk fast, there would be blood on the streets.

The county police car hurried silently in their direction. Aaron yelled, "Thank God." The two gangs tried acting credulously as the police slowed down and crept up. The police officer shined his spot light on the young men as the rival gangs moved inconspicuously in opposite directions. José turned his face toward the light after making eye contact with the police officer. He quickly realized it was Officer Bailey, the same officer who had pulled him and Aaron over, the same day he was shot. José did not like cops, did not want to be near a cop and preferred to keep his distance. But something told José to flag down Police Officer Bailey for help. It was not street protocol; you were being a snitch, a police informant. The cop car leisurely turned the corner onto Aaron's and José's block as Police Officer Bailey and his partner moved slowly away from the danger. On Aaron's cue, Aaron's old gang ran as Officer Bailey rapidly whipped around the corner.

Juan headed straight toward Aaron waving a gun in the air shooting. José could not move, frozen in time. When the excitement settled, Juan lay immobile in a pool of blood at his feet. José hollered out for mercy as he dropped all the candy he had purchased and ran to save his younger brother. He looked his brother's killer in the eye. He was cold and heartless. It was like a movie slowed down less than seconds; the murderer's expression said a thousand words. "Kill or be killed." Without another thought, he dove near Juan and climbed on top of him, in an attempt to cover his brother's injuries as the members of his old gang ran beside him shooting at Aaron's old gang.

People who normally staggered in the drug infested streets were scarce, scattered as bullets moved about in every direction. The streets of America turned immediately into the streets of Iraq as opposed gangs shot intensely in one another's direction. Sirens moved in but by the time rescue teams arrived bodies lay still. Bullet holes plastered on the near by cars. The window of a local business was shattered. As police units, fire trucks, and emergency vehicles paraded the streets, blocking the traffic in both directions, the streets swelled up with by-standers.

Trustee Jordan and Maria looked down the streets from their homes at the bright lights as they dance off the houses on the block. Maria walked down to Trustee Jordan. "What's going on?" Maria asked in her heavy Spanish accent. Trustee Jordan looked deeply in her friend's worried face. Fear raced through their bodies as they felt the danger surrounding their children.

José rocked back and forth on the ground as he held on to his lifeless brother. The blood of Juan spilled into his crying brother's hands as; an emergency unit technician squatted closely to José's Bible. She checked Juan's pulse confirming José's fear. Aaron cautiously walked out of the door of the Bodega and stood over José. He began to look at the curbside filled with limp bodies. Men in uniform forced Juan out of José's hands as Aaron struggled to keep him calm.

The emergency unit sirens and light traveled down the street loudly. Trustee Jordan and Maria, frantically hollered and screamed as they raced to toward their sons. They embraced their children as they moved off to the side. Unaware of Juan's death, they tightly tried to understand the horrific situation.

Rebecca Stanton as well as news reporters from across the nation posted nearby, announcing the death of seven, four wounded. Minutes after both Trustee Jordan and Aaron walked through the door of their homes; Maria and José moments later had walked through theirs. "Oh, my God! Aaron." Trustee Jordan yelled for her son as Aaron ran to her, she was standing in front of the television watching the breaking news. "What happened?" She howled as she stood immovable in front of the TV.

José told Maria. She screamed on the top of her lungs. "Why?"

Part Twenty-Seven

The sun shined brightly. The summer was a couple of weeks away but it was felt like it was already there. The streets all around the town were full of people with long faces and flowers. The local businesses continuously discussed the death, which had taken place in their town a week ago; and the lives of seven young people. Police Officer Bailey and other men and women in uniform blocked the roads as the bodies were planned to proceed down the street from whence the young men had once played and walked about. The breath they once took for granted would stop early. The lives they had would no longer walk this great earth. So much sorrow and pain was felt from this tragedy. Seven families had to bury their sons. The phrase "Here today, Gone tomorrow," is on one of the national newspapers.

Pastor Money traveled east bound on Peninsula Avenue in Hempstead, down From Bishop Edgar A. Love H.S., where the march started. They headed south to U.C.G.S. Church. The streets were lined with mobs of well wishers. The family, Pastor Money, politicians and other national leaders from every Black organization locked arms and walked in memory of the young men who had died for no reason. Tears flowed and some fainted as a mixture of heat and pain took hold of their bodies.

The doors of the church were held open while seven thousand people tried to cram into a building that had a capacity of three thousand people. The young people of Rap Session sat on the left side of the church in a large group. All members of the family were led in and seated on the right side of the church. Mary Ann and Abraham sat with other well wishers in the balcony. Aaron and Trustee Jordan sat with José and his mother; and their extended family members. The pulpit was adorned with every leader of the community. Onlookers stood outside, down in the basement, in the vestibule, off to the side and in the balcony of the church; as the funeral service was announced over the loud speakers. The front of the church was decorated with an array of flower arrangements that carefully lined behind seven glistening caskets, with seven bodies that lay at rest. Not a space in the church was unoccupied. Still, there was an inadequate supply of air. The well wishers were not moved or fazed by the sweltering heat. They desired to see these young people; their peers, their family, their neighbors, their students, their friends and what could have been their own funeral.

Police officer Bailey and one hundred other officers patrolled the inside and outside of the church, in fear of gang retaliation. The police officers wore plain clothes but their familiar faces to so many of the trouble teenagers were ignored for a short moment. A truce had been made for the time being, while people paid their respects. The officers stood militantly around the sanctuary. If it were not for the friendly white officers, their presence would have almost reminded the on-lookers of the Spike Lee movie, Malcolm X. The Muslims stood obediently waiting for Malcolm X, to give them the order to move out.

Pastor Money gave his sermon after a long eulogy and the choir musically touched the souls throughout the world. "Every national news reporter is parked in front of this church waiting for a glimpse of a congregation in pain and mourning the death of these seven young boys. Every Black local and national leader has made an appearance and showed support. Black people cry all around the nation. It reminds me of the death of four innocent Black girls. September of 1963 a racially motivated bombing of Birmingham's Sixteenth Street Baptist Church, which resulted in the death of four innocent Black girls, was the lowest point of the Civil Rights movement in Birmingham and perhaps one of the darkest days in Birmingham's history. City authorities, never sympathetic to Blacks, did very little to bring the bombers to justice. Locally, the bombing brought the factional Civil Rights leaders together. Nationally, the bombing gave the movement not just a face, but four faces, four young, innocent faces.

How about the story of Emmett Louis Till? His abduction and murder in Mississippi in August of 1955, and the subsequent acquittal of his killers the following month, became not only a national story, but also put Southern racism into the international spotlight. These events became a major force in the advancement of the Civil Rights Movement. Some would even say they were the catalyst.

The difference between those stories and the story we are living today, NOTHING. What is the excuse for the death of these seven boys?" Pastor Money asked as he looked into the eyes of a congregation filled with young people. "What two things do the death of those four girls and Emmett Till, a young boy, have in common with these seven young boys? They were all Black young children and their deaths have become national. Will the death of these seven young boys spark a movement against gangs, enough so it will push to end gang violence as they pushed to move racism? Or will you do nothing?"

"Mothers who have lost their children to gun violence cry, today. Families who have sons and daughters fighting in the war are crying. Sons who live at a distance are thought of, today. People, who have children, are right now, thinking about their child's future. Parents who have not hugged their children in a while are hugging their children. Sons who had planned to do wrong have stopped to think for a moment. People, America is crying; and why?

We are crying because we all know not one but seven young men did not have to die. We are hurt because somewhere deep inside of our bodies, we feel as though we could have done something that could have saved these seven boys lives.

I can preach until I turn blue in the face but tomorrow is not promised and today is only here for a minute. So, when will you realize that God's purpose for you is to find it in your heart to serve him some way, some how, in your own special way? The way we can serve him is by bringing young people to Christ and away from the streets. If those young people you know haven't listened to you before, if they had no other reason and if they can't figure out a reason, then today gives them all the reason to accept Christ. Young people I want you to come forth and accept Christ today, if you are going through something, if you are struggling with this kind of pain you feel right now, if you've belonged to a church and have left for whatever reason, if you are having problems in school, if your parents are not there for you, if you have no friends, if you can't find a reason to live, if all you think you have is yourself in this world, if what you are dealing with is too heavy to bear, if the streets is your family, if your family is your problem, if you are a single mother, if you have been to jail, if you can't find a job, if you feel you need to carry a gun for protection, if you think you have no future, if you belong to a gang, if you have lost someone and your mad at God, if Christ is not in your life, come right now!"

The church roared. The people on the streets shouted for joy; Pastor Money and the dignitaries stood in astonishment. The families of the deceased painful cries turned into praise and glory. Rebecca Stanton, the news reporters began to take a different spin as they too realized something powerful was happening all around the world. The spirit overwhelmed even the anti-Christ, the thug, the hopeless, the future murderers, the impossible, the discouraged, the unpromising, the failures.

Deacon Taylor sat in the front of the church in a designated corner. A touch from a hand on his shoulder caused him to open his eyes from his silent prayer. He looked upwardly from his wheel chair as he sat peacefully taking in God's presence. The tears rolled down his crumpled face as he youthfully wiped them away. He cried even louder in joy as his eyes went from seeing Lucious to the bundle of joy he held in his arms. Lucious carefully placed his daughter, in the arms of Deacon Taylor. Emmanuel, José, Isaiah and one thousand other young people had joined Christ, from U.C.G.S. Church. The gangs let go of their colors and around America it was being reported of an influx of young people joining churches in every state, in astounding numbers. For the day the world had deemed as a day of sorrow, turned into a day of hope and joy.

Part Twenty-Eight

The graduates of the class of Bishop Edgar A. Love H.S. sat eagerly awaiting to conquer the world. The graduation began with the Bishop Love Gospel Choir synchronized voices. Mr. Petillo, the Principal, asked his good friend Lucious Bell, to be this year's guest speaker. At first Lucious was ready to turn it down, but eventually accepted. After his publicized car accident and the death of his wife, Lucious became a local celebrity. Everyone wanted to see and meet the Blessed child of his, who made it from the car wreck but lost her mother. The audience was honored to hear what he had to say after months in exile from the small community.

Without a memorized or well scripted speech, Lucious walked up to the podium. He already prayed for his words to be guided, not to give him any glory or recognition. As every eye gazed at him with great anticipation, he began to speak. "Some of you may know me from the restaurant in town where most of you have broken bread and have eaten the best soul food in New York," He said with a proud grin. I know some of you because we live in the same community. Some of you may know me through my wife, who taught here at this school." Lucious tried to limit his emotions. As Rebecca Stanton reporting for CNN and other news reporter blocked the right side of the auditorium ready to report the state of gang violence in America.

"My wife was killed a couple months ago in a car accident. Her death and our accident were reported in the papers and television. Some of you may remember my family from that. But I want to give thanks to God, publicly because my daughter's life was spared. She was protected by her mother's womb and she and I survived. That's not how I want you to remember my wife, me, nor your graduation. But I wish to have a moment of silence, not only for my wife but also for the seven young people who were killed. They were your classmates and although my wife's death was an accident, theirs wasn't. They died because of gangs and gun violence. Let us not forget the GANG KILLERS that swept our nation last year. After all the smoke cleared, we were left with two teenagers on death row and on their twenty-first birthday, they will probably be put to death for sadistically killing over fifty other teenagers while involved with gangs." The audience silently took a moment. This is something we should not be happy about because I do not believe the execution of these two gang members will bring back those fifty other young boys. I want to go on record and with all the reporters here today by saying, I do not believe in the death penalty. I do not believe in an eye for an eye. Violence against violence doesn't bring back my wife or give my daughter back her mother. I rather celebrate knowing every child in America for Graduating, like these students in the back of me then to celebrate any man or woman being put to death by another man."

Matthew 5:38-42 "An eye for an eye and a tooth for a tooth. But I tell you not to resist an evil person. But whoever slaps you on your right cheek, turn the other to him also."

"I say this because you have to live your life to the best of your ability. You have to go out and conquer the world and the only way to conquer anything in life you must first fight your own demons. And when you do and you will, I do not want you to forget us at Bishop Edgar A. Love. Like you, I graduated from Bishop Edgar A. Love H.S. and aimed for the skies. One of the most important things I learned from graduating from this high school is not to burn bridges that you may have to cross another day. You will need more than yourself to get across them.

My mentor, Deacon Taylor who is here today, once said the deepest words a person could ever tell another person; to the point, if you miss the message, you will miss your blessing." Everyone paid close attention as they tried gathering what Lucious was saying. "He said **The Truth of the Matter is: Our lives are predestined. Everything that happens in your life has already been set in stone but when you find your purpose in life, you'll set out for greatness. You will stop thinking about yourself at that point and set out to make a difference in the lives of others. But in order for you to see your purpose, God is going to take you through a series of tests; some small but some not too small. You must hold on tightly because when you come out of the darkness (whatever you are going through), you will see the light; and at that point you will understand why you have been placed here. You'll see that some things are out of your control; and that which is in your control you'll give only your best.**

I spoke to my good friend, my classmate and your principal of Bishop Edgar A. Love H.S., Mr. Petillo, to let him know what I could do to help our young people and now I would like to tell you." The audience already silent and moved by his speech could only wonder what more Lucious could say. "I'm announcing that my restaurant will be closing it doors, for good," He said as everyone made a dreadful sound in disagreement. "By next year, we plan to open a youth center with a roller skating rink, a two lane bowling alley, arcade games, pool tables, a kitchen, computer room, basketball court and gym. It will be a brand new facility." The students went wild before he could close his speech. "Do not just thank me, but thank my wife who did not die in vain. Through her I've learned my purpose. I have received an outpouring of letters and donations. The seven young men who lost their lives did not die in vain either, because the world heard their cries; and donations to this cause overwhelmingly came in to our town. The Mayor moved mountains for the space to be allocated to you; and close to the high school. Pastor Money of U2 Can Get Saved Church donated more then half of the money to get the project off the ground. So, you have some friends to thank."

Deacon Taylor along with Mary Ann and Abraham indulgently listened to Lucious speak. Lucious had given a short announcement; which was appropriate and aligned with Emmanuel. He was the valedictorian and his long speech would turn into a sermon. Emmanuel walked up next after being introduced by his school principal and all the educators willing to deal with the "task" of educating young Black youth. He stood on the stage and looked out to the audience, at his parents, Aaron and his mother, José and his family, Lucious, Deacon Taylor (his grandfather), Pastor Money and then at his classmates and teachers. He stared at the speech he had immaculately prepared. But he was silent. Everyone stared in his direction as if they were trapped in time, waiting for the first word to come from his mouth. Without another minute to waste, Emmanuel began to speak from his heart as he addressed the graduating class. "Dr. Taylor once told me, he used to think it was **not impossible but hard** for him to become a doctor. It was not impossible but hard for some of us, including myself to get to this point. We walked to and from school but Dr. Taylor walked 7 country miles to school and 7 country miles back home. He almost died as people were being lynched around him, just to get an education. But his long walk made my journey much shorter and easier. I've learned that it was called the **Transferring of Grace.** Each generation must transfer their honor to another generation. The old generation leaves something behind to make our lives a little better.

1 Corinthians 15:10 "But by the grace of God I am what I am: and his grace which was bestowed upon me was not in vain; but I labored more abundantly than they all: yet not I, but the grace of God which was with me."

Emmanuel continued to say as the crowd followed his every word. "I use to not care about whether I would graduate and would always complain about my messed up situation. I told myself what the world has shown me, 'WHO CARES'. And at that point God spoke to me and showed me, He cared. I made up my mind to graduate but to graduate with honors and with a scholarship.

See, I knew I could do it, even when the world around me said differently. God told me, 'so what you just met your mother three years ago. It does not make a difference.' I met my father and grandfather last year. But I knew I had come from greatness," Emmanuel said as he looked down at Deacon Taylor. "I always knew I had come from greatness, but it was not confirmed until I met my mentor Mr. Lucious Bell and my grandfather, Deacon Dr. Taylor. He was one of the first African-Americans to move into Hempstead with his mother and siblings. He was the first African-American to teach at Bishop Edgar A. love High School. He was the first Black principal of this great high school; and it was not until he was told his students could not pray that he packed his bags, turned in his resignation and instead of enjoying life, chose to teach at a parochial school.

I figured out my purpose in life at an early age because of him. *I can't change the world but the world can change me if I allow it. I can make a difference.* So, when I rejoice and brag about the goodness of God, you all will now understand. I would not have been your valedictorian if it were not for God's grace. God blessed us all."

The audience looked at their program as Pastor Money pushed his old friend Deacon Taylor toward the lower podium and microphone. Pastor Money was the last speaker on the program. "You all did not think you were coming to church; you thought you were going to a graduation. Isn't God good?" The audience applauded. "You know I did not know my good friend and my classmate from Eutawville, South Carolina had a grandson." He said to Deacon Taylor and the crowd. "Family," this is Deacon, Dr. Taylor whom you have heard so much about this afternoon." The crowd stood to give a standing ovation to a well deserving person. Pastor Money motioned for the audience/congregation to be seated as if he was back in the church. For another minute they continued to applaud Deacon Taylor, not until Pastor Money spoke, did they settle into their seats.

Truth Of The Matter

"If I knew we would be having church, I would have invited my ushers to help take up a collection. And some of you need to go back to church because when a preacher says, have a seat, he means have a seat or ya'll just want me to talk longer. Because the energy from a congregation causes a preacher to talk too much and you all have a lot of energy. That's good." Pastor Money along with the audience laughed.

The auditorium had unnecessary movement taking place. Pastor Money was displeased and quickly scolded the audience as if he was in his own church. "Your valedictorian told you how he just met his folks but some of ya'll whose children barely graduated probably invited the most family. You know there was a cut off limit but you still came with forty people. You've invited Aunt Bo, who doesn't know how to act when you take her out, Uncle Butch, who can't wait to get a cigarette and a drink and your neighbor, who your family fought all year. Now, sit down and be quiet." The audience laughed so hard, it took Pastor Money another minute to get them quiet, again.

"The message you have received today should make your soul feel good. You know when you have received a good word; you stop thinking about the time and your stomach." The audience again laughed. "You know when they asked me to come to give this graduating class a few words of encouragement; I asked God what could an old man say to this generation? I did not know what I was going to say, until now. After listening to Mr. Lucious Bell and knowing he sat where you sat." Pastor Money said speaking to the graduating class. "After listening to your valedictorian electrifying speech; and wondering why this young man is not sitting in my pulpit. But it is great, knowing not only is he sitting in this graduating class but also he is the grandson of my good friend, Dr. Taylor. He will be preaching at my church for youth Sunday.

I knew Dr. Taylor was coming but I thought he was coming to support me not knowing his grandson would be graduating today. These young men, Mr. Bell and Mr. Jones spoke so highly of my friend. I was told by God to ask Deacon Taylor to come up to speak to you because he has your words of encouragement.

Deacon Taylor looked up at Pastor Money in tears and lost for words. "I think this is the first time Dr. Taylor has been at a loss for words." Pastor Money said to the crowd. Deacon Taylor was passed the microphone as the audience began to weep with him in joy. Deacon Taylor put in a little silent prayer before speaking. As he began to speak the power moved throughout the packed auditorium.

"I have been honored by every organization you could think of in my lifetime. But I have never been so honored to see Mr. Lucious Bell and my grandson, as well as all of these young people put forth what so many of us have died for. Some of you are so happy to have made it to this point. If there is one thing you should be grateful for it is that you are graduating.

I remember when I was told years ago our children could no longer pray aloud. They removed God's presence from the schools. I thought from that day, there was no hope for our young people. I never stepped foot back into this building and I was hurt. I am here today to declare that after you have lost seven classmates and a teacher in one year, we need prayer and God's presence in this building more so now than ever before." The crowd applauded loudly.

"I listened to my grandson talk about how my generation had to walk seven country miles to school and seven country miles back home." He chuckled. "Well for those of you who've never been to the country, a mile seemed even longer when your only scenery is cotton and tobacco fields. Despite my hardships, there are three things I want you to realize we have in common in obtaining our education. We had to walk to get it, we had to have a good pair of shoes to do so and it was a matter of life and death to get to this point. Let me explain what I meant. First, my generation walked 14 miles in comparison to your 1. We wore old, holey shoes, which were passed down from our siblings. You wore $150 pair of sneakers. We had to get past the White racist Klan's men or get lynched and attempt to walk the same path going back home. You have to get past Black and Hispanic men who happen to be your neighbors, who are in gangs that do not kill because of the color of your skin but because of the color of your clothes.

You have a purpose in life and are called to do great things in life. In this very audience right now there are some of you who have no clue what you will do after today, some of you who think they have their entire lives planned out and some of you who are simply surprised that you have made it thus far. I want you to know that people are depending on your success, your leadership, your determination, your perseverance, your happiness, because you will someday have to pass the torch on to someone else. What if slaves stopped believing and had no faith? What if there was no civil rights movement? What if your grandparents did not tirelessly fight for you? What would have happened if your forefathers decided to stay in their condition, stop living and just died? Where would you be?

See, yesterday, we knew our purpose early in life because someone was taking away our right to vote, our hope to live, our faith to go on, our will to do better, our fight to persevere and our education to think for ourselves. Men were being lynched and women were being raped. You were worth less than a dog and treated as property. If you did not know your purpose in life after all of that, then it was not worth living.

Someone in this graduating class has said to him or herself, what if life is just too hard, if you've lived on public assistance, if your family had no real place to call home, if you had no clue where the next meal was coming from, if you had no dad or mother, if you had to join a gang for protection, if no one ever cared about your well being, if you barely made it to this point, if no one ever did anything in your family, if no one has ever given you a break in life, if you come from nothing, if all you have been taught to do is hustle, if the streets is all you know, if you have no clue why you even exist, then your purpose in life is to make sure your children and your children's children never deal with the same things in life. As Emmanuel said, **transfer your grace** to the next generation. We should not have to always start from scratch in life and if we do, make sure no one after you is left to figure out what you already know. I will tell you what I tell everyone I care dearly about. I want you to tell someone you care about. Mr. Bell has already told you but I will say it again, **The Truth of the Matter is: Our lives are predestined. Everything that happens in your life has already been set in stone but when you find your purpose in life, you'll set out for greatness. You will stop thinking about yourself at that point and set out to make a difference in the lives of others. But in order for you to see your purpose, God is going to take you through a series of tests; some small but some not too small. You must hold on tightly because when you come out of the darkness (whatever you are going through), you will see the light; and at that point you will understand why you have been placed here. You'll see that some things are out of your control; and that which is in your control you'll give only your best.**

Why are you waiting? Go and reap your rewards in life and let nothing stop you from making your dream a reality. Do not give up so easily on things. If it doesn't kill you, it should only make you stronger and bring you a bigger blessing. Follow your heart and discipline your mind. God Bless you all." The auditorium stood on their feet and erupted with applause as many wiped their tears.

Graduation caps flew into the air simultaneously. Lucious got up from his seat in the packed auditorium. He walked over to Deacon Taylor and his family with Baby Sarah wrapped in the blanket; his wife had passionately sewn during her pregnancy. Trustee Jordan and Aaron rushed over from where they were seated in the auditorium. Trustee grabbed the baby in a motherly way from Lucious. José and his family, Emmanuel, Isaiah and his family, Shemaiah and her family as well as Aaron and twenty other graduates and their families circled around Deacon Taylor as they thanked him and Lucious for caring about the youth. "Don't thank us." Lucious said as he smiled.

Emmanuel was given a full scholarship to attend Virginia Union Seminary School, to become a preacher. Shemaiah did not allow the gown to hide her individuality by wearing military honors on her cap and traded her blue gang colors for a yellow ribbon on her gown to show support of the troops in war. She expressed herself by dying her hair a natural color and decorating her lips with a neutral colored lipstick. She plans to attend a Fashion School.

Isaiah was recruited into the United States Navy. José planned to attend Nassau Community College, inspired to become a teacher and work in his community to continue to rid the streets of gangs.

Aaron and Trustee Jordan attended the graduation show support. He graduated from his parochial school and was accepted to Norfolk State University.

Abraham and Mary Ann were working together on their lives, through Christ. They agreed to start a new friendship.

Lucious had plenty help with Baby Sarah. He enjoyed fatherhood and running the youth center. He was serving his purpose in life.

Deacon Taylor after discovering the fountain of youth looked as if he would live to be 120 years old. He wasn't going anywhere. Because of his rejuvenation, Pastor Money has asked Deacon Taylor to come out of retirement to be the Director of the Church youth programs.

APPENDIX

A Collection of Articles Written By, Bruce K. Davis, Jr.

John 14:6 "I am the way, the truth & the life; no one comes to the Father but through me."

The articles I have written were compiled a few years ago. Every time I faced an uphill battle, I prayed to God and then I would express my thoughts through my writing. The articles led me to me write ***Truth of the Matter.*** From writing these editorials, I was not only able to express myself but I was empowering myself not to accept anything less than greatness.

Like Jack Nicholson's character Jessep said in the movie, A Few Good Men, "You can't handle the truth." The articles are facts based upon the authors view point. The truth is God's word, and his book is called a Bible. Like the young author, everyone has a story and an opinion but not always the truth; and the ***truth is what matters***.

Can you handle the truth?

Eye of the Storm

Mark 4:39 "He arose, and rebuked the wind, and said unto the sea, Peace, be still. And the wind ceased, and there was a great calm."

At first, everything around you is peaceful and calm but your spirit is not sitting well. You feel something catastrophic is soon to happen. You have received all the signs but you have ignored them. Your mind has acknowledged the red flag that has gone up in your brain. Unfortunately, your natural senses are telling you to prepare for the worst; hold on and grip tightly. This ride is going to be very dangerous and can cost you your life. The storm has arrived. You tell yourself, *it is not as bad as it seem.* Your world of comfort is being turned upside down. You think you are going to die. You began to give in but you continue to hold on for dear life. You pray like you've never prayed before. You are hoping God is listening. You began to think He is not going to come through but He answers just when your grip has loosened and you completely let go. You are screaming and crying with your eyes closed then you open your eyes and there the sun is prancing on your drenched body. After you have fret and dread the worst, God saw fit to save you.

When you have just come out of a storm you will have an appreciation for life. You will know what it meant to be touched by God and you will serve your purpose on this earth. You will know what it felt like to have an Angel watching over you. Some storms/situations may seem as though they will never end but the rainy season only last for a short amount of time. The new season is surely to come. The spring is the beginning of new life. A bad situation only comes for a season. You are in a storm for a reason. God wants to change something in your life. You might not want change but **Change is Gonna Come** whether you want it or not. **The Truth of the Matter** is Change is inevitable:

In the process, God is:
1. Developing a new image to help raise you to the next level
2. Matching your image on the outside to the image on the inside
3. Developing your <u>character</u>: who you are when no one is looking.
4. Building your faith and hope

5.   Removing your "Deaf and Dumb Spirit" so you can remember scriptures and speak his word with meaning
6.   Making changes in your life
7.   Carry you through a transitional phase of your life
8.   Teaching you a thing or two
9.   Allowing you to see your own capabilities, strengths and weaknesses
10. Fighting your battles

Psalm 37:23-24 "The steps of a good man are ordered by the LORD: and he delighteth in his way. Though he falls, he shall not be utterly cast down: for the LORD upholdeth him with his hand.

Through my struggle to becoming a better Christian, I have learned something in finding my purpose. I learned I would not have received God as I did, if I was not at my lowest point in my life. I heard from God much better when I had nothing, than when I had everything. You cannot do it without God. He giveth and he taketh it away. When the storm is all over, the sun reappears, the birds are chirping, the streets are dry and the people are on foot.

1.   How well did I treat you, in the lowest point in my life?
2.   Did I treat you like you had anything to do with my struggle?
3.   Was I mean to you, when I had nothing or was I acting like I was better then you when I had it going on?
4.   Did I befriend you?
5.   Did I belittle you?
6.   Did I ever speak to you with kind words or was I moody all the time?

Luke 6:37 "Judge not, and you shall not be judged. Condemn not, and you shall not be condemned. Forgive, and you will be forgiven."

Don't Get Lost, Use Map Quest

Luke 15:4-7 "What man of you, having a hundred sheep, if he loses one of them, does not leave the ninety-nine in the wilderness, and go after the one which is LOST until he finds it? And when he has found it, he lays it on his shoulders, rejoicing. And when he comes home, he calls together his friends and neighbors, saying to them, 'Rejoice with me, for I have found my sheep which was LOST! I say to you that likewise there will be more joy in heaven over one sinner who repents than over ninety-nine just who needs no repentance."

If you are as hard headed as me then let me give you the footnotes. We think we know it all and learn everything, unfortunately the hard way in life.

1. Begin to read the Bible
    ♥The Bible is your road map. It does not mean you will not get lost but it will give you direction from start to finish. When you begin to read the Bible, be specific. What do you want from God? If it is wealth, then look in the <u>concordance</u> of the Bible. Look up wealth, prosperity and rich. You should read scriptures that relate to what you are dealing with and what you are asking of God. Read the Parables another time.
2. It is just a test
    ♥1 Chronicles 29:17 "I know, my God, that you test the heart and are pleased with integrity.
3. Write a mission statement, business plan of your vision on how to succeed
4. Recognize
    ♥ You are not the only person going through a crisis
5. Find strength and refuge in a Bible teaching church.
    ♥The church should teach you the Bible in a practical way. The scriptures should be broken down to the point where you can relate from where you are in life.
6. Look at the company you keep or your scenery
    ♥Who you align or associate yourself with as well as the negative company you keep can disconnect the ***transfer of grace.*** A Negative environment harbors negative behaviors. Your family or friends can be just as bad as the enemy you

keep your distance from. The job that just pays the bills could be hindering you from thinking of owning your own business. The rat hole you live in and pay double the amount of rent or double the taxes then people on Park Avenue could be the reason your health is taking the turn for the worst. Change your association and location.

7. The harder you fight to accept the issue, the longer the struggle
8. Grandma knows best.
   ♥Sit beside the oldest member of your church; they have wisdom and the most faith. They have lived your life.
9. It is only your fault, if you do not act upon it
   ♥You know what the problem is, yet you do nothing about it. Or you have done everything by yourself but when are you going to realize, you can't do it by yourself? Faith doesn't activate until there is some sort of action on your part.
10. You are not less of a person or Christian, just an imperfect human.
   ♥You may careless how you are perceived but becoming a Christian should make you want people to see the good in you. They know your evil side; why not work harder at people seeing God in you.
11. Do not lose hope or faith
12. Do not expect much from family or the best of friends
   ♥You are setting yourself up for great disappointments.
   ♥Expect much from God
13. Shame and Pride will only decrease your chances of positive results
   ♥When you have no Shame or Pride in what you do, you show others how much you care. But if you can careless about life, then you are not being fair if you are raising children because you are decreasing their chances of living a positive life.
14. Build a thick skin because people talk
   ♥You already have layers of thick skin because people talk too much about nothing. Give them something good to talk about.
15. Get out of the way & let God do His job
16. Listen to uplifting music and watch comedy or action movies- NO DRAMA
17. Other people around you depend on your positive changes
   ♥Your children or spouse are some examples. Why you do not have any of the two is another matter.
18. It is OK to cry but don't scream.

♥Learn how to have an indoor voice. Everyone should not know all your business.

19. Anything that you may think will have fast results and may help take the problem away will only make matters worst
20. Get over it.
   ♥Understand you are being *forced* to make changes in your life. So, why not get the life you deserve.
21. There is a reason.
   ♥God can get across to you at your lowest points in life
22. Life is predestined.
   ♥God knew this would happen at that very moment.
23. Pay attention to your health
24. Prayer has power
25. Smile.
   ♥It is only temporary, just a learning lesson. Instead of trying to kill the person who made you angry, kill them with kindness. Nothing makes your enemy more satisfied then you frowning. So, SMILE.
26. Take mental notes, so you will know what to do next time
27. Give God the glory.
   ♥You will praise Him at your lowest point in life but how about at your highest point in life?
28. Serve your purpose in life
29. Help someone else find their purpose
30. Continue to read your Bible.
   ♥Whenever we travel and do not know how to get there we go on-line and refer to "Map Quest" (Bible). Life is the same. Before you begin to travel down a road you have never been before, refer to the Bible. Know where you are going before you find yourself lost, alone, without gas, no money, confused and trying to back track you steps. Don't just get in the car like the majority of us men and don't ask for directions because you know what happens 99% of the time. Yes, we get lost. So, check with God.

John 16:33 "I have told you all this so that you may have peace in me. Here on earth you will have many trials and sorrows. But take heart, because I have overcome the world."

Roman 3:23 "For all have sinned & fall short of the Glory of God.

Righteous Indignation

Ephesians 4:26 "Be angry and not sin: do not let the sun go down on your wrath."

"We are supposed to feel righteous indignation when we see something wrong. God meant us to feel bad when we see wrong. It is a sign of spiritual health and a good conscience. If we are so understanding and permissive that we can watch wrong and feel nothing there is something seriously wrong with us. God himself is annoyed when he sees evil. It was in righteous indignation that Jesus threw the moneychangers out of the temple. If we were to see someone sadistically beating some other living creature to death it would be natural and right for us to be angry. In the same way if we can sit and allow our Black youth watch immorality glamorized and romanticized videos on television without feelings of anger and righteous indignation it is a sign of spiritual sickness. If we can sit and listen to philosophies and negative viewpoints illustrated on the Don IMUS Show that are in deep conflict with the teachings of the Bible and Christianity and not feel anger then something is truly wrong. God expects us to get angry about wrong actions; not only for our own sake but for that of children. If a father allows his young teenager son to mistreat young women and doesn't get angry about it he does the son wrong. The young man needs to see his father react in righteous indignation. Only then can he respect and believe in his father. The young man intuitively knows he did wrong and anger on the part of the father is the only proper reaction. Not to get angry is to condone, needless to say rewarding with a smile for his actions is worst. Not to get angry shows a perverted mind and heart. The same would be true if the father were to catch his boy stealing, or using profane or offensive language."

Proverbs 29:15 "To discipline and reprimand a child produces wisdom, but a father or mother is disgraced by an undisciplined child."

1. What wrong doings upset you at times?
2. Are there things happening around you that you feel are wrong?
3. What can you do to help the matter?

Shut Up and Lead
"The Cry of Young Black People"
Ephesians 4:11 "An He gave some apostles; and some prophets; and some evangelists and some pastors and TEACHERS."

As a thirty-two year old Black man, an entrepreneur; a person who has served this country in the military; a father, a husband, a person who has grown up in the Black community; graduated from one of our great all Black public schools; was a member of a traditional, ultra-conservative church, a voter, a civic participant and as a tax payer, my heart goes out to all of us as young Black people.

Marching on Washington Voters vs. Driving to Local Mall Voter
Proverbs 12:27 "The lazy young man does not roast what he took in hunting, but diligence is the young man's precious possession."

Out of 35 million African-Americans living in the United States, how many vote? Everyone expects us as young people to understand our right to vote but when it comes down to it, older Blacks are making just as many excuses as young Blacks. Young Black men and women, who have served time in jail, still are unaware that they too are able to vote. Whose fault is this? Our young people have no clue what some of our "old Black organizations" stand for or if they still exist. Ask any Black young child, what does N.A.A.C.P. stand for or mean to our young people? They could not tell you because everyone is still talking to one another about how it was when they marched on Washington. If Black children of today saw Black adults picketing our schools as their grandparents did in the 50's and 60's the misconduct and mishandling of school funds would quickly cease. You would not have to ask us what does the National Association for the Advancement of Color People mean to us, because we would know like you once knew and its membership would grow. If the young Black children like to fight in schools then why not use that negative energy like your blood, sweat and tears were once used and turn it into something positive to bring about change? What happened to us marching in thousands for a great cause?

Preventative Programs (help us now) vs. Rehabilitative Programs (help us later)

Proverbs 28:20 "A faithful man will abound with blessings, but he who hastens to be rich will not go unpunished."

The entire nation is making money off us from the time we are born as Young Black people. The social worker receives a paycheck, to try to keep our "Black Baby- Having Babies" in check. The school receives more money for each child, regardless of over crowding. For every child with some sort of dysfunctional, mental or social behavioral problem in your school the check gets bigger. The police department (White and Black Officers) are getting paid overtime to protect African-American thugs from other criminal minded African-Americans in what is considered some of the worst neighborhoods across America. The correctional facility gets six figure salaries to keep us from killing one another while already locked up. The big time companies get free labor while we are incarcerated, the liquor stores and drug dealers are all set up to help us drink and smoke away our problems. Crooked politicians who do not have our best interests in mind make great dollars to keep our vote from counting; and the name brand clothing lines make money by making a child think they really can afford the same items as that Hip-Hop artist. With all the money being made on our children's failure then why would anyone want to invest in any type of **prevention** program? The money will stop if there is no problem to continue to solve. It would be more rewarding for big business if we just continued with **rehabilitating.** Basically, what we are doing is placing a band-aide over an amputated limb without cleaning the wound. Then we wait to see how the wound affects the body or if the person is still alive after years of going without treatment. We know there are major problems without our Black communities across America but like Hurricane Katrina, America waits.

Not-for-Profit Organizations in the Black Community vs. The Church

Mark 8:36 "What shall it profit a man if he shall gain the whole world and lose his own soul?"

If there are so many not-for-profit organizations getting federal funds to help the Black community with our social issues, then why are Black kids situations, worst? Every not-for-profit organization have no problem being the "hub" of our Black community for our social dilemmas and have no problem finding the federal funds but the Black Church which should be the focal point is struggling financially? Every Black civic organization, youth center, social development agency in the community should come from the heart of the church.

Our government will not assist religious institutions in bettering the Black community with their major social and economic programs. The **truth of the matter** is Black people have to sow a seed into our Black communities. You reap what you sow.

There is an evil force that is assembled to enforce separation between church and state. The idea is to keep God's people from having too much authority; by not relinquishing their power. So, they allow ungodly institutions to set up shop and under-service our community.

The only not-for-profit organization in America is the church. So, instead of every organization having its own agendas and the bulk of their funds going toward a building, why not pay rent to one of the many churches in the community, use some of their space for the betterment of our community and take the funds being used for a building and put it toward the organizations mission statement and purpose. We nee more of us to do it from the heart and not because of the funds.

Love thy neighbor vs. Who is that?
Luke 10:27 So he answered and said, "You shall love the Lord your God with all your heart, with all your soul, with all your strength, and with all your mind, and your neighbor as yourself."
Jesus tells the parable of the Good Samaritan Luke 10:27-37

If a person is not a member of your church or civic organization you probably would not even realize that you are all neighbors. Why is that? It should not take an act of God for you all to realize one another's existence. As a young Black person I can only learn how to love my neighbor if you show me how you love yours.

The Latino Community vs. Black Community
1 John 2:9-11 "He who says he is in the light, and hates his brother, is in darkness until now. He who loves his brother abides in the light, and there is no cause for stumbling in him. But he who hates his brother is in

darkness and walks in darkness, and does not know where he is going, because the darkness has blinded his eyes."

I cannot complain about Latinos in "our" community because they support each other, they stand by one another and they clearly understand who their "American-enemies" are. We fight each other and then try to understand why our children are killing each other. If you've lived on the earth long enough you know that hate is taught. Then why teach it? All that we have been through and become, why is that we are still **struggling** and Latinos are **advancing?** I'm not mad at them but I'm mad at us, for they fight the way I was told we once did. Why are they building barriers on the Mexican border and not on the Canadian? Every time you come into contact with a European immigrant, do you wonder if that person is illegally in America? No, because you believe everything you hear, without finding out the **Truth of the Matter.**

<u>Teaching Black Pride vs. Keeping Knowledge to yourself</u>

Deuteronomy 6:7 "You shall teach them diligently to your children, and shall talk of them when you sit in your house, when you walk by the way, when you lie down, and when you rise up."

In the Black community if you have a great career, better education and buy from the imported section of the supermarket you consider yourself elite. Yesterday, the doctor lived next to you and today he can't be seen standing near you. Well I have one thing to tell you. They see us all the same way but are just impressed by you. An old wise man once said, "When you have impressed someone do not gloat because it was not meant as a compliment but as an insult. They were not impressed as much as they were surprised because they did not expect much of you in the first place."

It cannot always be about the resources as to why we withhold knowledge from one another. We have the money because we spend too much to begin with. So, why are we segregating ourselves like "Willie Lynch" once showed slave owners how to do? I know. You've been accepted and I have yet to be. As a young Black man, embrace me, teach me and I will soon show the world my purpose in life.

<u>Segregation vs. Desegregation in the Public Schools of America</u>

Mark 6:11 "And whoever will not accept you nor receive you, when you leave from that place, shake off the dirt from under your feet as a testimony against them. Assuredly, I say to you, it will be more tolerable of Sodom and Gomorrah in the Day of Judgment than for that city."

I graduated from a predominantly segregated Black High School in the 90's but in the 50's we fought to desegregate American Schools. The United States Supreme Court ruled Brown vs. the Board of Education among America's most significant judicial turning points in the development of our country. It dismantled the legal basis for racial segregation in schools and other public facilities. It was monumental, when it was declared that the discriminatory nature of racial segregation violated the 14th Amendment to the U.S. Constitution, which guarantees all citizens equal protection of the laws. This helped lay the foundation for shaping future national and international policies regarding human rights.

Almost 60 years later since America declared our public schools racially equal. The Bush Administration implemented the "No Child Left Behind" and still we are worst off in our educational institutions then before the 50's. This is 2007 and we are still dealing with racial division in our public schools. Jena 6 in Louisiana recently dealt with six Black students that were wrongly arrested for beating up a white student. This is an example of our American Institutions that harbor racism and segregation that is still prevalent in our public schools.

Question: Are we better educated? Are we still segregated? Did the generations before the 50's learn more from the educators who lived in their neighborhoods and understood their issues? It seems as though our young people not learning until they attend a Historically Black College?

W.E.B Dubois vs. Booker T. Washington

Luke 12:48 "For everyone to whom much is given, from him much will be asked; and to whom much has been asked of him they will ask more."

The average young Black might say: "I have not received much, so do not expect much of me." If I were a Young Black man with no skill and no education, what would Black leaders such as W.E.B. Dubois and Booker T. Washington see me as? W.E.B. Dubois felt Blacks should educate themselves and Booker T. Washington believed Black people should have a skill. What would they see me as ...."Not worth debating.

Grateful vs. Unappreciative
1 Timothy 4:12 "Let no one despise your youth, but be an example to the believers in Word, in conduct, in love, in spirit, in faith, in purity."

From the Young Black People of Today, we thank you for not giving us the proper tools, equipment, training, skills and education to continue on this journey. We thank you for giving up. We thank you for not teaching us how and why we should vote. We thank you for allowing them to remove prayer from schools. We thank you for not taking us to church and showing that your strength came from God. We thank you for not eating healthy food as a family at the dinner table, but introducing us to fast food and causing us to deal with obesity, Diabetes and heart related diseases at a young age. We thank you for taking a rest. We thank you for enjoying the wealth of today because of the hard work of yesterday. We thank you for allowing our schools to be misused and abused by unqualified individuals. We thank you for not taking us in and most of all we thank you for not teaching us what you were taught.

Giving Thanks vs. Not Caring at all
1 Thessalonians 5:18 "In everything give thanks; for this is the will of God in Christ Jesus for you."

One thing I can hope for is that my children mean it when they thank me, just as I did when I thanked my parents. If you are still fighting for young Black people, we thank and salute you. If you have not put in the work, time, effort, energy to make things a little better for young Black people, then SHUT UP AND LEAD.
Quote: A great leader must first learn how to be a great follower.
1. Are you a leader or compulsive complainer?
2. How are you helping the situation or are you hindering others?
3. Do you feel you can help then why are you just standing there, get busy.

Registered Christian
"The Cry of Young Christians"
Proverbs 11:14 "Where there is no guidance, a people falls; but in an abundance of counselors there is safety."

The Churches in the town were very politically connected; at least where I grew up. The Elected officials depend on the Black Churches to pull them through, in towns that are majority African-American. But what if the politician valued your vote as a registered Christian voter? What would America do if Black, White and Hispanics were registered as a Christian Voters? Who would our elected officials worry about pleasing? What issues would be on the topic of their agendas in comparison to what they fight for, today?

As a Young Christian, the older Saints I admired were all politically attached but could not be bought or sold. Although, my parents are Democrat's, it didn't mean I had to vote the same way. My issues are not the same as my parents. My problems cannot be handled by any one person but what God did tell me, is to vote for the person who has a Christian heart. If politicians would elevate God's power over their own then everything else would fall in line.

Everyone was in the closet as a "Christians." What drove Blacks to abandon one party most closely associated with civil rights to join another? Which party truly helped people of Color? Does the Republican Party have higher morals or do the Democrats have the best interest of African-American, as so many of us suggest? Why are we not as strong as a Registered Christian Voter, first? No, we do the unthinkable and vote which ever way the wind blows. Just another reason to divide the Christian votes.

So, what was so strange to me was while everyone quietly claiming to be "Christians", on paper everyone was boastfully speaking out for their party lines. Maybe, just maybe, this was why no one wanted to discuss the "voting issues" to Young Black Americans. Some were Democrat and some were Republicans but what do you consider yourself first and foremost? Before anything else I'm a Registered Christian."

I grew up in a house with a family who made it their business to teach me, how to vote. It was profound to grow up with so many professional Black people. All the faces of Color worked to bring change to community. They all discussed and felt the same on every issue i.e. church, education, careers, family, community and living prosperous lives. But I found it very odd for a group of African-American people who once fought so hard to vote and yet not talk to the younger generation on the most important issue, Voting.

While I was growing up, the Black Church did not allow anyone running for office in the church, during election time. You had to have the best interest of Christians. You would not be swayed to vote any other way. You would support the side, which supported the "Word," family values, Christian beliefs, prayer in the schools, faith-based programs and God.

The people, who surpassed and prospered, were those of God. Everyone else in the community had to align themselves with the word of God or connect with a person who could get them a job. As a teenager, I watched God's people run the voting registration. The church leadership checked and balanced the elected officials. People understood who Christ is before they knew a local politician's name.

Some of us do not know who or what to vote for. Today, going into the voting booth is like taking a test. It is harder to vote with yesterday's equipment when you are accustom to today's technology. Half of us vote because the person is Black. But are they a Christian?

Young Christians hardly ever look at the issues. So, guess who come out winning because of our confusion in Black America? The Unsaved politician, who can careless about our salvation, is the newly elect. If they cared about your salvation, they would be concerned with your happiness. Some Party members have the best interest of Christians. But we are not worried about what they are but "Whose" they are.

Mark 12:38-40 "Then He said to them in His teaching, Beware of the teachers, who desires to go around in long robes, love greetings in the marketplaces, the best seats in the synagogues, and the best places at feasts, who devour widows' houses, and for a pretense make long prayers. These will receive greater condemnation."

By dividing the vote amongst the community does nothing but harm us as a whole. We should stick with the Christian Party and make everyone vote God like, first. There is only one issue that should matter most to an elected official, is whether their community is serving God. If that was the case all our battles would be resolved.

We would like for you as a Young Christian Voter to know what to look for in a candidate:

1. Person who abstain from every appearance of evil.

2. Understands the importance of building great relationships.

3. Respect your elders.

4. Don't pretend to be humble by smiling a lot and ignoring things.

5. Don't take vengeance.

6. Publicly Rejoices in the Lord!

7. Publicly Prays.

8. Publicly Give thanks to God.

9. Publicly Worships God.

10. A person of good character, not short tempered and trustworthy.

Proverbs 14:7 "Fools have quick tempers and no one likes you if you cannot be trusted."

What a Young Christian Voter should do to please God:

- **Love God**
- **Love yourself**
- **Love your family**
- **Love your friends**
- **Love your neighbors**
- **Love your enemies**

I dare our young Christians to show the rest of America, your purpose. I suggest you take your electrifying energy, little money, small amount of time, effort, big voice, book knowledge, refreshing ideas and build a platform. Team up with like minds, other Christians and start working together for God, in your communities.

Ecclesiastes 5:8-9 "If you see the oppression of the poor, and the violent perversion of justice and righteousness in a province, do not marvel at the matter; for high official watches over high official, and higher officials are over them. Moreover the profit of the land is for all; even the KING is served from the field."

1. Do you vote?
2. Do we just vote or become active bodies in the election process?
3. Which election effects your community the most, the local or national elections?

Black Organizations vs. Black Church

Luke 11:17 "But He, knowing their thoughts, said to them: Every kingdom divided against itself is brought to desolation; and a house divided against a house fall."

The Black church has been the pivotal and focal point in Black America. Black Americans have been silently and secretly communicating through the Black church, since the beginning of time. Through the Hymns and Songs we mapped out freedom.

During the civil rights movement meetings across America were held in the Black churches to liberate communities and people. Pastors, community leaders, organizations and the people came together for a common purpose. Our differences and reasoning were irrelevant. We had a purpose and if we did not stay on course more lives would be lost. But today with every organization and every denomination in Christianity we all get confused and forget that we all have the same things in common. Because of our doubtfulness we often questioned Black leadership's. We tend to go off in different directions trying to fore fill our common goal separately.

Acts 4:32 "And the multitude of them that believed was of one heart and one soul; neither did anyone say that any of the things he possessed was his own, but they had all things in common."

But some of the oldest community organizations in the black community are not going to exist in the future. Why? The Black churches and other Black organizations needed to work better together in enrolling our youth. In some cases, our children do not become apart of anything but gangs. Some churches are stuck on yesterday and do not accept change to help young Christians better understand Christ. I had one Pastor tell me, "I do not allow these organizations in my church because everyone that is apart of them are not always Christian. I told him in a respectful manner, "not every person in the church is a Christian."

This is a **RECOVERING GENERATION**. This generation is just now getting on their feet. After decades of Crack Cocaine and Aids, the children of the 80's and 90's are moving in the direction of change. Younger people are getting involved in community activities, they are voting, and they do care about their community issues. They are forming new organizations that answer to their needs. Instead of thinking the young generation is not involved in any civic organizations asks some of them what non profit, civic organizations they are involved in? You will be surprised to know the oldest organizations only exist in your world but the younger generation is running out starting new movement. Meanwhile, organizations that have been around for over a hundred years are dying because of old Black leadership. There is no new blood, new vision or new ideas.

Now, if a young person cannot tell you about some of the oldest organizations in their community then tell me how affective that organization is to young people? Ask any teenager, which gangs are in their neighborhoods? Black teenagers could tell you how to identify gangs, what part of town gangs control, who the gang leaders are and what type of pull gangs have around their way.

The Black church is the foundation of the Black community and the civic organizations are there to bring communities together. Believers should be ready to teach non-believers why it's important to become one, but shutting the doors only gives them more of a reason to conduct a civic organization meeting out of wicked ways. Some churches do not know how deal with the communities social issues, nor are they equipped. The Black church and civic organizations ought to combine their forces to combat the social neglect within the Black community. Until, we start fighting this war our youth are entrenched in, I guess we should stop asking questions, we already know the answer to.

1.   Why aren't our Black teenagers being productive in the community?
2.   Why are our young people not going to church?
3.   Why are our children joining gangs and not a local civic organization?

Colossians 3:21 "Fathers, do not embitter your children, or they will become discouraged."

The **Truth of the Matter** is: Every church should have a dynamic youth ministry and it is imperative that every organization should have a strong and vibrant youth department. It is vital to a church to have YOUTH ministry full of life. Your young people should be in charge and actively conducting meetings. The church is a place where our young people need to learn leadership. The young church members should give time to local civic organizations in their community as much as they do in the four walls of the church. When a young person participates in their community and in their church that person gives balance to their lives and enhances their community. The problem is the congregation depends on their Pastors to fight all their community battles. Everyone is too busy and not involved. Just as we do with Black organization monthly meetings, we do with our school board meetings, town meetings and church meeting, we do not go.

So, people feel the church should only deal with the Bible. I agree but the church is God's Temple and the Black community's foundation. If the church does not help clear the smoke in the community then the average person will continue to exhaust themselves. People are dealing with major problems and are not open to receive their blessings. Sit in any civic organization meeting and figure out the average age. If the average age is 65+ then you have a problem and a lost generation. If you have an over flowing number of young people then your organization accepts change. If you consist of senior citizens then you need to make some changes or you will not have a chapter in the future. I have failed to mention one last thing: If your organizations biggest achievement in the past year was an annual dinner then you have not achieved much for the Black community. Don't get mad at me, I'm just telling you the TRUTH.

1. How productive can we all be if there are hundreds of organizations popping up with small memberships and working to benefit small problems?
2. Is your church or organization full of life?
3. Does the church or organization you are involved with accept change?

The "N" Word

Proverb 18:21 "Death and life are in the power of the tongue: and they that love it shall eat the fruit thereof."

The "N" Word is used as a hateful word towards African-Americans. But it is now used by the grandchildren of those same people who once had to turn a cheek. How did it come to this place? How did a new generation succumb to carelessly using the word? Why would they refer to each other as the "N" Word? Were they not taught the true meaning or cared less? Is the next generation so fortunate and Blessed in life from their forefather's fight that they could not see passed the bling-bling?

1 Corinthians 13: 11 "When I was a child, I spoke as a child, I understood as a child, I thought as a child: but when I became a man, I put away childish things."

As a young Black man, this is how I have come to explain it to myself, to my children and to the generation after me. This is how I saw the ugliest word come into the lives of a generation that hardly knew themselves. This is how I broke it down. We are not making any excuses for the word being used but trying to understand why the word is being used. We need to use this information to remove the word from the mouths of our young people. Make no mistake; the word is ugly and full of hate.

The civil rights movement had made a great impact on the lives of African-Americans and other races. We finally reaped in the 70's everything that was sewn for us before 60's. Black music changed from rhythm and blues to funk and disco. Everyone began to enjoy the "American Dream." Marijuana was considered an enhancer rather than a drug. Sex was a "Sexual Healing," as Marvin Gaye said. Everyone was having unprotected sex with anyone and everyone. Black momentum was stronger than ever. The music had a political message. The civil rights movement went from non-violent to the next generation of Liberators who saw a need to fight harder and more aggressive for African-American rights. Affirmative Action was enforced and the doors of opportunity seem to give more African-Americans a better way of living.

But the 80's quickly rolled around. Black men had just finish fighting and dying in the Vietnam War. Those that made it tried to live a decent and prosperous life until crack cocaine and Aids had finished off what was left of the already tired Black Will Power. The new Black men of Liberators were killed or incarcerated. The Black family, women and children were now dependent upon a welfare system that enslaved generation after generation. This took us back to slavery when the head of the house, the father was sold off and separated from his family. Now, Daddy is locked up. Mama is cracked out and the children's up bring were no longer the responsibility of the birth parents but the state.

Grandma who had been the most faithful was thrown back into motherhood and fatherhood. She was forced out of retirement, after raising her own children to become the head of the house. The new breed of African-Americans were no longer hidden but exposed to the harsh world. Family values, morale, hope, love, understanding and religion is replaced with frustration, anger and self-hate. A new generation was born with hate for their mother, father, family, God and themselves. Now, a group of people who had once aged gracefully had aged overnight, lights turned back to darkness.

In the early 1900's civil rights leader Booker T. Washington endorsed the "Negro" word. We called ourselves "Colored." In the 60's James Brown song, "I'm Black and Proud." We called ourselves "Black." In the early 80's Rev. Jesse Jackson said we were African and American, thus the name "African-American. In the 90's and 2000 the Hip Hop culture has embraced the negative "N" word and has referred themselves as "NiggAs." This has taken us back to 1700's when the slave master used the word to refer to African slaves. The word has carried with us for centuries it connotation of hate. America and the world have come to know the word as a derogatory meaning toward people of Color and yet our new generation has permitted such a dark word to have life by allowing it to flow from our mouths.

Nigger is defined as stupid, violent, a lazy person with no self respect or regard for family, ignorant, slow moving, uneducated, childlike traits and has no moral character. National Association for the Advancement of Colored people (NAACP) has twisted the arms of Merriam-Webster to change their dictionary definition by no longer using African-American; at the same time.

People of Color were beat, raped and robbed of their rights. We were considered to be less than human. Our rights as a born American were stripped from us and we were seen as third class citizens. This country became the richest and most powerful country in the world on the sweat and blood of People of Color. Being that our right to vote was illegally taken away from us; we had no voice in politics. What we had was "Faith."

Willie Lynch teaching was and still is alive in our communities. Our fathers and grandfathers then were called "Boy." Our people were constantly reminded of our place in this so-called civilized society. In keeping a person of Color in check, racist individuals tormented us with the most degrading and derogatory word that pieced through the skin of the strongest Black man. When a Black man was addressed as such, he kept from having any eye contact by lowering his head to keep from showing his anger. Our people were put down to the level of a four-legged creature when they were subjected to this word. Unfortunately, our young generation has two different meanings to the "N" Word. Society has even helped our children define the word in two different forms:

My Nigga- Friend of a friend

Nigger- An ignorant person.

But make no mistake; the word is what it is, degrading and hateful. Now in 2007 politicians and other Black leaders would like to remove the word by locking anyone up, who uses the word. As much as I disagree with the "N" Word being used, I disagree with legislation passed banning the use of the word. I believe this law will only increase the imprisonment of our Young Black People and used against us in the end.

In the 80's everyone wanted stiffer laws to get rid of crack cocaine, a drug plaguing our communities. Our leaders helped enforce the Rockefeller law, which was only used to lock up one group of people, poor Blacks. Now, we want to turn around and pass a law banning the "N" Word to add on to the teenager sentence who is serving ten years for selling drugs and another two years for using the "N" Word in the presence of a white cop. Are we serious? When a law is imposed upon one group of people does not necessarily rid the use of the word but add fuel to the fire. The nature of the law is admirable but the implications of the law will only contradict what it is trying to achieve in the first place.

Instead of investing our time into this law, how about we invest our money in campaigns and ads on the same media outlets that allow glorified celebrities to use the word and teach our children how to disrespect one another. It is easier to pass a law, then to really teach these young people. "These young people should know better?" So you say as a person from the civil rights. The TV did not raise your generation and music had meaning and a message during your hay days. Still, the record labels and movie studios continue to use the word and encourage our children to use the "dumb word."

Proverbs 12:18"There is one who speaks like the piercing of a sword, but the tongue of the wise promotes health."

Do you think anyone beside Young Black People are going to be affected by this law because if so, you are sadly mistaken? How many Michael Richard's (comedian from Seinfeld Show) you think are going to be sitting beside your Black grandchild in the penitentiary? How many Black comedians are still using the "N" word? Thanks to one of the best comedians of all time, Richard Pryor, the word became alive.

Our Law makers pushed forward to pass the Rockefeller Law. Twenty years later we have incarcerated over half of the next generation. We are fighting to get rid of this law we once thought helped our race but was only was used against us. Now, we are trying to turn back the hand on the clock. But remember one thing; laws only help those in the position to make laws. If we are not Black Judges and Black Lawyers in these courtrooms, then the only one who laughs last are those who are truly not affected by the situation.

Older African-Americans want to quickly blame this young generation for setting our people back centuries because of the use of the "N" word. The Hip-Hop generation is a generation with plenty of hope. This is a lost and forgotten generation, who truly pulled themselves up from their "boot straps." They have learned to have determination and preservation. During the birth of this generation, the ***transfer of grace*** had stopped at the door. No one had planned for their future and when Daddy died, there was no "WILL" but disturbing memories. All this generation could do in the mist of crack cocaine, AIDS, injustice, war, oppression, decrepit communities, no parenthood, no leadership and hardship was PUSH. This generation as 50 Cent said, "Get Rich or Die Trying." Hell was at their doors and being poor was not acceptable.

Revelation 3:17 "Because you say, 'I am rich, have become wealthy, and have need of nothing' and do not know that you are wretched, miserable, poor, blind, and naked."

The Hip-Hop Generation had created an empire worth billions. More millionaires in the Black community have come from America's Black Ghetto's because of the Hip-Hop industry. Now, we are empowered. We have the buying power, the influence to change, the perseverance and the determination to get what we are after. We have the microphone, all the attention, fame, glory and fortune but not the responsibility. We want to "keep it real." Real is when you drive up to the "Hood" some kid on the street is emulating the character or brand you have created. Everyone wants street credibility.

1 Corinthians 15:33 "Do not be deceived: Bad company corrupts good characters."
The majority of the Hip-Hop generation does not believe in censorship. So, if we do not believe in censorship then we must take ownership. We cannot have it both ways. We are responsible of our young people. The Hip-Hop generation has to own up to the words that have a <u>cause and effect</u> on the lives of other people. The words coming from some of our Hip-Hop artist influences the youth. As Jim Jones (the sociopath preacher led 900 people in his congregation to a foreign land and convinces them to drink poison cool-aide). As President Bush words influenced other Nations to go to war. Should these leaders not be held accountable for affecting the lives of others through the influence of their words?

Proverbs 15:1 "A gentle answer turns away wrath, but a harsh word stirs up anger"

Words are powerful and can be used to manipulate. Our young generation has been manipulated into thinking the "N" word is acceptable. Our young generations of African-Americans have been influenced by the power of media to turn a repulsive word onto themselves. Our youth are taking more negative information into their spirit then positive and not aware at such a young age on how to differentiate from bad and good. We should hold ourselves at a conscience level. We have to counter act the ads on MTV and BET Video Shows with a clear message, and then I believe we will see the affect on why a word with so much hatred can be removed from the mouths of so many young peoples vocabulary.

It is not against the law to use the "N" Word but we want our young African-American children to know that it is against your ancestry, against your own people, against your seed, against who you are. The word draws division amongst a nation, which makes it a law against humanity. And because the "N" Word is so hurtful and full of hatred it can only be against God.

Matthew 12:30 "He that is not with me is against me; and he that gather not with me scatter abroad."

1.   Do you believe the lyrics used by some rap artist are   based on how they see the world or a figment of their   imagination?
2.   Do you believe the music that is heard around the world, which is written, produced and generating billions of dollars promotes the use of the "N" word by our youth?
3.   Is music powerful?
4.   Do you believe words have power?

Luke 6:45 "A good man of the good treasure of his heart brings forth good; and an evil man out of the evil treasure of his heart brings forth evil. For out of the abundance of the heart his mouth speaks.

Generational War
Build bridges and eliminate the gap between Generations

Hebrews 6:12 "Then you would never be lazy. You would be following the example of those who had faith and were patient until God kept his promise to them."

The **Freedom Fighters** lead the fight and fought hard for the rights of all Americans. They were born during the Harlem Renaissance Era **(1900-1950's)**. They left the most for the generations that came after them. They were willing to die for a cause and believed in a good fight. They fought for injustice. They were not the most educated of all generations to come but the generation with the most heart. They had more faith then any of their off springs and with very little they push forward. They did not believe in prosperity for today because it seemed unobtainable but waited on the Lord. Tomorrow was to come and today did not matter. **What matter the most was their faith in God.** What they had endured did not matter; they would be rewarded in the end.

Baby boomers were born **1946-1964**. They broke barriers and were now living the great dream. The boomers were more educated than any previous generation in American history; and thanks in part to advances in medical care; they are projected to live longer than any generation before them. They worked the factories and industrial plants. Out of this generation formed the clear understanding of what were now middle class people. They have had more jobs dealing with their hands, they were skill laborers. Baby Boomers would remain at a job until they were considered retired and with a pension. They found it hard dealing with the fast paste of technology.

Luckily they did not have to deal with major job cuts from America's biggest corporations; as these companies either discontinued thousands of jobs, moved the other thousands of jobs over seas and easily required a formal degree that was once unachievable. Baby boomers, children (**Generation X, 1965-1982**) the grand children of the Freedom Fighters. Generation X grandparents paved the way and their broke barriers. But the job market dried up on Generation X. Let us not mention, **Generation X**, had no chance getting in the door because the positions were still filled with Baby Boomers who had no intentions in retiring for another thirty-five years, plus. Now, the same company required from Generation-X a formal degree, no health benefits, less pay, hourly instead of salary and you must be willing to move to India, for a managerial position.

In order to land a job in America, you would have to move out of the country. When jobs are removed from America to a place like China or India this is called **outsourcing**. This is also the major reason why Generation X feels the need to fight illegal immigrants because they need to blame someone for the lost jobs in America. Americans should not blame illegal immigrants because they are out of work but our government. There should be a law against companies outsourcing American jobs.

Our grandparents (Freedom Fighters) could not move into white neighborhoods and our parents (Baby Boomers) seized the opportunity but the grandchildren (Generation X) is priced out of the house market. Those born 1983-1995 in the Black community were raised on a large scale by the grandparents (Baby Boomers, grandchildren) due to the influx of crack cocaine and A.I.D.S that plagued our communities.

Now, the next generation to follow has been placed on God's great earth and our capitalistic society already calculated the buying power of eighty million lost souls. The media, corporations, music industry, movie producers and the government are ready to profit off our children. These companies are obsessed with the youth culture's buying power. The largest generation of young people since the '60s is beginning to come of age. They are called "*Microwave Generations*" because they're the genetic offspring and demographic echo of their parents, the grand children of the baby boomers and the great grand children of the freedom fighters. Born between **1982 - 1995**, there are nearly 80 million of them, and they're already having a huge impact on entire segments of the economy. They are spending faster then they can make it. They are the "*microwave generation*", they expect to receive their desires immediately without putting forth the time to earn it. And as the population ages, they will be become the next dominant generation of Americans.

Matthew 6:24 "No one can serve two masters! You will like one more than the other or be more loyal to one than the other. You cannot serve both God and money."

The Microwave generation have watched Twin Towers collapse, terrorism at its highest on American soil, Hurricane Katrina. Yet, our young people still deal with racist comments from Imus calling Rutgers women basketball team, nappy-headed whores, after school job being replaced by illegal immigrants, Virginia Tech massacre, Columbine massacre, American schools go down, gays get married, elected official get caught in indecent sex scandals and children pornography; prayer removed from their schools, corporate America brake financial records and still insist on having more. Young celebrities go to jail, get killed or paid even more money for bad behaviors. HIV plagued their parents and cripple their families, crime walk into their homes by the inter-net, priest get sued over child molestations, unprecedented weather changes, lack of great national leadership, heavy influences from unclean media, single parents govern their homes, behavioral problems be pacified by drugs, high school students gun down their peers, war from every angle of the globe at one time, the "N" Word come back from the dead in the worst way, less communication, more rights, more sex, more tolerance and no supervision.

What did today's generation do to any of their predecessors to cause such hostility against them? The Freedom Fighter and Baby Boomers are displeased with Generation X and the Microwave Generation? They see Generation-X and the Microwave Generation as: slackers and don't want to work hard at anything, do not care about themselves or their future, hang out on corners because they have nothing better to do, live at home longer and are frustrated, hopeless and cynical. Some may agree but the **truth of the matter** is Generation-X and the Microwave Generation does not want to work harder but understands the process. The next generation plays hard and works less. In 1997 five million businesses were started nearly under age 25. The next generation is constantly being downsized by Boomers and has to work double to prove themselves in Corporate America, where there is no longer job security. They are not afraid to challenge authority. Unlike Baby Boomers who stuck it out at work even if they were unhappy. The next generation is very willing to pick up and leave a job that does not satisfy them. They are more health-conscious than previous generations.

2 Timothy 2:22 "Flee also youthful lusts; but pursue righteousness, faith, love, peace with those who call on the Lord out of a pure heart."

Truth of the matter is: we are still dealing with racism, segregation, unequal justice, less faith, and less family togetherness but these viscous cycles can not be broken without the younger generation learning from an older generation. The older generation has to be willing to accept change and new ideas; incorporate old traditions with new visions. Until, this is possible we will all lose because one generation wants things to remain the same and the other generation wants things to change over night.

1. Will God grade us as a group or individually?
2. Are you busy fighting older or younger people in your church or organization?
3. Are you open to new ideas and fighting old tradition?
4. Are we incorporating new ideas with old traditions?
5. What are you doing to stick to the mission of the church or organization but bring new things to the table?
6. Have your organization been operating the same for the pass fifty years?
7. Do you have a large number of young people involved?

Author's Closing Remarks & Benediction:
<u>A Change Is Gonna Come</u>

Proverbs 24:16 "For through a righteous man falls seven times, he rises again, but the wicked are brought down by calamity.

This book was written, while at my lowest point in my life. At that point in life, I heard God best. It was then, God was able to use me and inspire me the most. I realized at that time, when things and people failed, Jesus Christ came through. He placed people in my life to help get me through the hard times and rather than complain about the situation, I listened. Otis Redding said everything in one song, "A Change Is Gonna Come."

The Truth of the Matter is: Before you get to your lowest point and you find yourself dealing with overwhelming problems; and you think you have no where to go, look for the oldest church member in your congregation and hold on for dear life. Don't let go. Visit that elder at their home as a gesture of good faith and offer a plant as a gift.

Revelation 22:2 "In the middle of its streets, and on either side of the river, was the tree of life, which bore twelve fruits, each tree yielding its fruit every month. The leaves of the tree were for the <u>healing of the nation</u>."

I was told by an elderly usher in the church where I grew up, "always give a person their flowers before they leave this earth." Find the old and faithful, the person who has that old time religion and the strongest foundation. An Elders' faith is untouchable because they have been through the fire and back. They will inspire you more than any other person in your life. They will breathe hope and inspiration into your life.

Like the plant you offer as a gift, you will grow in the hands of the old and faithful. Soon, you will be astonished by your growth. Your newly found, old Christian friend will talk to you as they do with their plants. They will feed you with knowledge. They will place you in the best place, where God will be able to shine His light upon you. Your old and faithful friend will watch you grow and keep an eye on you and when you begin to wither; your old Christian friend will nourish you back to health and pluck dead things from you. And if you look like you are about to die, your old Christian friend will uproot you and replant you with a new foundation that will help you begin to grow, again. Your old and faithful friend will show you how take a piece of your new found growth and share your love with other people.

Everyone always takes a piece of a healthy plant from an old and faithful home but no one has ever taken a part of a dead plant. Other people will want a piece of you when they see you are growing beautifully in Christ. They will ask you for advice on how to grow and how to live healthy in a world, where trees (Christian people) are being cut down. Where can I go to grow? First, go to God. Second, go to the front of the church and sit beside the old and most faithful person. The people sitting in the back of the church are still guessing, still wondering and still asking themselves whether they should believe in Christ or not. God has a place for his most faithful people. Walk with the faithful and watch your faith grow. It is the best way to receive the **Transfer of Grace** into your life.

The old and faithful might not have won every battle but they won the war. They have the scars to show and they have walked away smiling. We cannot understand their joy because they are not bling-blinging, driving a Bentley, living in a mansion or carrying a "Black Card" or "Black Berry". We can learn a lesson if we are willing to take one of their classes about life. They have learned patience because they raised a family. They are loyal because they understand long lasting friendship; appreciate life because they saw death take love ones and understood forgiveness because they dealt with racism. They know how to build good relationships because they went to church. They appreciate being rich because they were poor. They enjoy living long because they lived healthy. They understand love because of marriage. They understand diplomacy because they have been in a few wars. They appreciate the land of opportunity because they remember what it was like not to have any. They understood making sacrifices because they knew nothing was greater than God's examples with sacrificing His only begotten Son, Jesus Christ. They know the **Truth of the Matter** because they read their Bibles.

How Can I Get Saved? It is as easy as:
Roman 10:9 "If you confess with your mouth the Lord Jesus and believe in your heart that God has raised Him from the dead, you will be SAVED.

Galatians 6:18 "the grace of our Lord Jesus Christ be with your spirit. Amen."

For book ordering information visit
WWW.TRUTHOFTHEMATTERBOOK.COM

For Further information contact
Bruce Davis, author @
E-mail: brucedavisbooks@aol.com
Myspace.com/brucedavisbooks

About The Author
Bruce K. Davis, Jr.

He and his wife, Tiana Jade Davis are Ministers-in-training and under the "Word of Faith" leadership of Senior Pastor Leroy Woodside at the Father's House, in Raleigh, North Carolina. Along with their two children (Bruce III, 3 years old and Brooke Kennedy, 1 year old), they are busy helping build God's Kingdom.

He joined the U.S. Navy to make a difference in the world; to see the world through his own eyes. He opened a restaurant to break bread with new found friends. He became apart of the NAACP and Omega Psi Phi, Inc. to stand for something. He was a student at Norfolk State University to help prepare him in life. He married for love. He had children to continue a legacy. He gets, because he gives. His fellowship with other Christians is a tool used to remain strong in Christ. He joined church to learn more, worship and strengthen his relationship with God. He believes because he realized how God's grace has been given to him. He recognizes the power in prayer because he has seen the evidence. He thanks God daily for answering his every prayer and taking time out of His busy schedule to talk.

Upcoming Book:

"SINFUL GREED":

Mekhi Higgins and Robert are cousins, who have grown up together but in different circles. They realize their different worlds are not so different when it comes to survival and success.

Robert is an all American successful marketing associate in a well respected firm. His professional success has caused him to forget his Bible toting foundation. Mekhi is trying to place his life back on the right track by getting "Saved" while serving five years in a state prison. He is released into his old environment all the while trying to mentally and spiritually go in the right direction. But Mekhi is finding out as much as he tries to be a changed man, his environment has not changed and it's causing him to lose hope and faith.

As they set bigger and better goals on their journey to success, they find themselves running for their lives when documents belonging to the world's number one villain are stolen. This all occurs in a breath taking, non-stop action, suspenseful, thrilling, comically ingenious story that takes place between the two boroughs of Brooklyn and Manhattan. Robert and Mekhis' separate but equal world's merge into one, when the only color that matters is green.

One Last Thing

I have been involved in the church all my life, but I didn't actually start to study God's word until last year (2006). Although, I do not know God's word as well as I should I am excited and celebrate my growth. As I was writing this book I would look up each scripture using the concordance of my bible. I was ashamed to admit that I have been going to church for over 20 years and didn't even know how to get to the different books of the bible. When I finished writing this book "Truth of the matter", I had over 450 pages. During the process God told me that I needed to confirm the passages in my book, with the scriptures from his. I childishly debated God before I submitted to what was being asked of me. Within 6 months, God lead me to each scripture and had me remove over 100 pages of irrelevant information. Finding a church that challenges my mind with the "Word" was a crucial part of my spiritual growth. When we first begin to develop a relationship with God, we have hundreds of questions. The first place to start looking for answers is the bible.

www.ingramcontent.com/pod-product-compliance
Lightning Source LLC
Chambersburg PA
CBHW030505260626
47157CB00005B/1665